Reunion for a Murder

The Rhonda Pohs Mysteries Book Four

Sherry Derr-Wille

Dedication

I would like to dedicate this book to my many fans who have been requesting murder mysteries for the past several years.

Chapter One

Rock County Homicide Detective Rhonda Pohs and her former partner, Phil Mason, were enjoying a rare evening off. Shortly after their case was solved, Phil took a promotion with a different police department. Starting with the new school year, he would be the liaison officer at one of the large schools in Madison. It was a great step up for him with better hours and more pay. The problem was it left Rhonda with a new partner.

Tonight, Rhonda and her husband, Mark, were hosting an impromptu picnic supper for Phil and his wife, Judy. While Mark worked the grill, Rhonda sipped an iced tea, enjoying the summer evening on the deck of the Pohs' home.

"So, how is it going with the new guy?" Phil asked, as they attacked the steaks Mark just took off the grill.

"About as good as you had it when I joined the detective squad. His name is Martin Alexander. Nice enough guy. He's been a cop longer than I have, but as a beat cop."

Phil rolled his eyes. "Well, you've been through three high profile cases. I bet it bothers him to have a woman supervisor, even one as experienced as you are."

"Yeah, my transition nearly did me in, so I should know."

Phil's wife, Judy, laughed at Rhonda's statement. "It seems to me; I heard Phil say these same things when you joined the squad. You'll see, I think everything will work out fine once the two of you get used to working together."

"Okay," Mark said. "Let's change the subject. No more shop talk. Since you've now got a cushy Monday through Friday job, what are your plans for this weekend, Phil?"

Phil stretched in his chair.

"You're not going to believe this. It's my class reunion. Only it's not like anything we've ever done before."

"You bet it's not like anything *you've* ever done before," Judy said. "Honestly, guys, this is the first one of his reunions I've been able to drag Phil to. He keeps saying there's no one there he wants to see, but this is the twenty fifth reunion. These guys are all getting older, it's hard telling how much longer any of them will be around."

"Yeah," Phil said, winking at his wife, "like we're so much older than you are. As I recall you were in the class behind us."

"So," Rhonda said, once she stopped laughing, "why a whole weekend for a reunion? Usually, those things are a one-night kind of thing."

"One of the guys from our class, Jackson Hayes, has a farm west of Clinton, and we're going out there for a three-day bash. On Friday night we're having a fish-fry. Jackson is supplying the fish and the rest of us are bringing everything else. Saturday night, we're having a catered dinner in his new pole barn, and on Sunday we're having a brunch, also catered."

"You'd think the food was the only thing Phil is interested in. What he isn't telling you is, for the rest of the weekend, it's pretty much a camp-out, complete with a couple of kegs of beer. It should be interesting."

"I was getting to that. Jackson even got Millie Peabody to come to be our keynote speaker for Friday night."

"Who's Millie Peabody?" Rhonda inquired.

"She was our class advisor."

"What an advisor she was," Judy added. "As I recall she was drop dead gorgeous. I think the boys were thrilled to death with it."

"That wasn't why we liked her, and you know it. It was a ball having her as our advisor. She was fresh out of college and green as grass. We got away with murder with her our freshman year. By our senior year she wised up to us. We still had a good time, but it was more productive."

"I'd say it was productive," Judy continued. "As I recall she left the same year you did. I heard it was because she left to get married, but the rumor was your class completely traumatized the poor woman."

"Whatever the reason for her leaving, seeing her again should be interesting. I don't know how Jackson tracked her down, but I'm sure glad he did. She was great. I think her name is Millie Beauchamp now."

"Somehow, I can't see you camping out and playing Farmer John,"

Mark commented.

"We're finally going to get to use that fancy camper Phil insisted on buying a couple of years back," Judy said. "I told Phil it was high time we got to do something with it rather than keep it out at my uncle's farm. I don't do sleeping in a tent and the fact Jackson has offered some of his outbuildings didn't appeal to me either. Several of us are bringing campers and tents. It should be very interesting."

"All I can say is I'm glad it's you and not me," Rhonda declared. "My kind of camping is a nice room in a posh hotel with room service."

"Funny, that sounds like living here," Mark teased. "I've been known to bring you breakfast in bed on occasion."

"He's got you there, Rhonda," Phil agreed. "There are days Judy really envies you. The only thing I can cook is Microwave popcorn."

~ * ~

Phil and Judy left Rhonda and Mark's house to go home and pack for the upcoming weekend. "I suppose you think I should be helping you with the packing," Phil teased as they pulled away from the curb and headed toward home.

"That sounds like a good idea," Judy replied. "If we both work at it we can have the camper ready to take out to the Jackson's place bright and early on Friday morning."

Phil didn't want to let it show, but he was excited about the upcoming campout. It had been years since he'd seen Jackson, and he hadn't kept up with most of the kids from his class, even though he lived less than twenty miles away from them.

On Friday morning, Phil worked hitching the camper to the back of his truck and checking the taillights to make sure everything worked properly. It was close to two when he was finally ready to leave for the farm to get his unit set up.

The farm was one of the larger operations in the area; there were at least three houses for the men who worked for Jackson, and the main house looked almost too elegant for a farm.

By four in the afternoon, everyone arrived, and Jackson gave a tour of the farm, including the barns, the milking operation and the machine sheds housing the newest equipment. To call him prosperous was a misnomer.

To Phil, Jackson didn't look much older than he had at their graduation twenty-five years earlier. At six foot two inches he'd maintained his lean body and six-pack abs. Even the gray at his temples didn't take away from his good looks.

The majority of Friday evening's activities took place around the well-stocked fishpond at the back of the property, up in the woods. Fish sizzled on the grills and the women spread out large bowls of coleslaw and other salads.

Being August, the bonfires wouldn't be needed for light until much later. They all sat around picnic tables spread with red and white-checkered tablecloths.

"I'm glad you could all make it here tonight," Jackson said. "We want this to be a fun event and, to start things off, I'd like to introduce Millie Peabody Beauchamp."

Millie didn't look much older than she had at their graduation twenty-five years ago. Her blonde hair was cut in a short and sassy style. She was still petite and very attractive. She'd always been the fantasy for most of the guys in the class and the announcement of her upcoming marriage had come as a real blow for them.

"I'm so pleased to be here tonight," Millie began. "I was so young when I started teaching and you actually made me feel as though I was a member of your class. Even though I'm living in Chicago now, it was an honor to be asked to come back tonight and see all of you. As you can see, there are several empty places at the tables and that's because there are several classmates who won't be coming in until tomorrow. For tonight, we plan to introduce several of the students from your class separately. Tomorrow night, several other students will be introduced and on Sunday, the remainder. It should be fun."

Jackson handed Millie an envelope and she pulled out the folded paper and scanned the names. "As I read your names, please stand so everyone can recognize you. Class president, Mike Krumpy, captain of the football team, Christine Wilson, oh dear, I apologize for the typo. That should be Christopher Wilson."

Phil was astonished to see a beautiful woman stand. "It's no typo, Mrs. Beauchamp," the woman said. "I had a complete sex change. I'm proud to have been the captain of our football team in high school, but in college I realized I really wasn't comfortable as a man."

Among the former classmates, there were gasps and whispers as they came to grips with the sexuality of their former friend.

"It seems we've all done our own things over the years," Millie said, regaining her composure. "Next, we have Debbie Collins Harrison Witt Dumont, head cheerleader,

Tom Coats, boy most likely to succeed, Suellen Mars Neuhouse, girl most likely to succeed, Evan Carmichael, waterboy for the football team, John Mallory, class clown, Kathy Granasee White, star of the senior class play, Marcy Allen Olson, valedictorian, David Olson, Boy least likely to succeed, Geri Arner Salizar, prom queen, Tony Carpenter, wrestling champion, Marshall Grant, editor of the school newspaper, Kandice Kane Whitaker, winner of the Betty Crocker Homemaker award and last but not least, Pete Potter, our quarterback."

With all the other students standing, there was a strange silence as no one got to their feet.

"I said Pete Potter, our quarterback," Millie repeated.

Before anyone could say anything, there was a scream from the pond behind where they were enjoying their fish fry. "Dad, Dad, come quick. There's a man floating in the pond. I think he's dead."

Immediately, Phil was on his feet running behind Jackson to the pond. As soon as he got there, he saw Pete Potter floating face up with a large gash on his forehead. By the color of his face and the amount of blood turning the water from clear to a pinkish hue, it wasn't hard for Phil to ascertain the man was dead. "Don't touch anything," he shouted. "This is a crime scene. Someone call 911."

"You're a cop," Mike said, "isn't there something you can do?"

"Not on this one, Mike. We're all suspects here. I can't even begin to investigate this murder."

"I've got 911 on the line," Christine said, handing the phone to Phil. "Maybe you should talk to them."

Phil took the phone and gave the operator the location of the farm. "This is Phil Mason, I used to be one of the homicide detectives for the county. I'd like Rhonda Pohs called in," he finally said.

He certainly didn't want any of the other detectives he'd worked with to be questioning, not only him, but also his classmates. Rhonda was the best and the only detective he trusted to investigate this and concentrate on every angle of the case.

"Is it true?" Millie asked, when she and most of the others gathered around the pond. "Is Pete Potter dead?"

"I'm afraid so," Phil replied. "Please don't come any closer."

He looked at the worried faces of his friends, then concentrated on Judy. He knew she understood what he did for a living, being she'd been married to a cop for over twenty years, but he still didn't want her to see such a gruesome sight. "Even though I don't have any crime tape, this is a crime scene."

~ * ~

Rhonda was just getting home from dinner with Mark when her cell phone rang. "Pohs here," she answered, after stepping into the kitchen.

"We've got a murder. They've requested you be the primary on this one," Sheriff Cantwell said.

After giving her directions to the murder scene, he advised her Martin would be coming to pick her up in about fifteen minutes.

"I can't believe it," Rhonda said as she ended the call and turned toward Mark. "The murder we're going out to investigate is at the farm where Phil said they were having their class reunion. I'm worried. What if our victim is Phil?"

"Something tells me Phil is the one who requested you. He can't investigate something that involves him. His just being there puts him under suspicion and you know it."

"I understand, but having Phil there and not being able to rely on him as my partner makes things difficult. It's going to be hard having to question Phil about what happened out there tonight. It doesn't help matters to have a new partner. I have no idea how he's going to react to my being the primary on this one. I mean, I worked on a lot of cases with Phil before I was the primary on the Adkins case. I knew how he was going to react to me. Martin is a complete unknown."

Martin arrived shortly after Rhonda changed from jeans and a tank top to a more professional summer suit. On the way out to the farm, she briefed him on the fact this was a class reunion for her former partner.

"Do you think Phil Mason is involved in this?" Martin asked.

Rhonda worked hard to keep her temper in check. "Hardly. He was in the wrong place at the wrong time is all. Maybe I should say he was in the right place. He knows how we operate. I'm sure he's already set up a place where we can talk to the classmates in attendance. If nothing else, he's keeping everyone calm. This isn't the ideal situation, you know. I'm sure several of the classmates are from out of town, so we don't have the luxury of being able to question them over the upcoming weeks. Everything will have to be done this weekend. I hope you're prepared for this being a long couple of days."

Chapter Two

The scene Rhonda found at the Hayes' farm was utter chaos. Tents and campers were scattered around the freshly harvested mint field. Red and blue lights from squad cars and ambulances flashed and the people attending the reunion were either in a state of shock or were crying.

It took only a moment for Phil to approach their car. Beside her, Martin seemed to be awestruck. In the past, he would have been one of the patrol officers responding to this emergency, not a detective investigating the murder.

As soon as Martin parked the vehicle, Rhonda got out and went to where Phil was standing.

"I assume you asked for us," she said, shaking Phil's hand.

She looked around to see where Martin was and smiled to see him hurrying to catch up.

"I wanted the best."

"You must be Martin," Phil said, turning his attention to Rhonda's partner. "I hope you know how lucky you are. I asked for Rhonda for a reason. She's going to teach you a lot."

Martin nodded, but Rhonda noticed a combination of irritation at playing second fiddle to a woman and apprehension about his first murder investigation.

"Where's the body?" Rhonda asked.

"Still floating in the pond. I wouldn't let anyone pull him in before you got here. Luckily, it doesn't get dark until much later, since we've had the forensics team out here taking pictures. As soon as you've assessed the scene, we can transport him to the coroner's office for autopsy."

Martin followed Rhonda to the edge of the pond. Rather than wade out to where the body floated, she assessed the situation from the shore. "There's little doubt about the cause of death."

"How can you say that?" Martin asked, his face a deathly white at the sight of the dead body before them. "Don't we have to wait for the autopsy?"

"We do, but considering he's floating face up, he certainly didn't drown, and the gash on his head isn't self-inflicted. It all leaves little doubt about the reason he's floating out there."

She turned her attention back to Phil. "What can you tell me about the victim?"

"His name is Pete Potter. He sells insurance just down the street from our former high school. He was the star quarterback. From what I've gathered tonight, he's not married anymore but he does have an ex-wife somewhere and they have a son living someplace up North. As far as who did it, I think you're going to have a hard time sorting through the characters here, me included."

"I take it you weren't one of Mr. Potter's best friends." Rhonda cringed.

She didn't like having to question her former partner.

"That's putting it mildly. I wasn't one of the jocks in high school, therefore not in his inner circle. I took more than one towel slap from Pete in gym class, but good god that was over twenty-five years ago."

"Sounds like normal behavior for high school kids to me," Martin said, his tone one of mockery.

"Of course, it was, but we all grew up," Phil agreed. "When he went into insurance, he tried to sell me one of the companies he represented. I had my own agent and didn't want to switch. The last time we talked, I mean really talked, not just polite conversation when we happened to meet at social gatherings, he was going on about his football exploits."

Rhonda nodded. She'd met a lot of guys who couldn't let go of the past and decided Pete must have been one of them.

"When I said I didn't want to talk about the past," Phil continued, "he changed the subject to insurance. I let him know I didn't want to switch carriers or agents for that matter. That was when he informed me, I never was a team player and since I didn't want to switch my coverage, he wasn't interested in working with me. That was the end of the conversation, as well as any relationship we might have had. It takes more than going to school with someone to make him a friend."

"I have to ask this," Rhonda said. "Was there any reason you might have wanted to see him dead?"

"Of course not. I didn't want to associate with him, but I certainly didn't want to kill him. I'm sure you want to record these interviews. I talked to Jackson. It seems his son has a recording studio in one of the outbuildings. The kid has everything set up so you can interview people there and get them all on digital recording. So as not to compromise the case, he said we could have our own people running the equipment and he'd show them how to use it. Gordon Chase from forensics is with him now going over everything."

The fact Phil took charge of the situation made Rhonda breathe a little bit easier. "Have you informed all these people they can't leave here?"

"Not yet. I thought it was best if you were the one to make it official, since I'm involved in this mess as much as they are."

Rhonda followed Phil back to the area where the attendees of the reunion were all sitting at picnic tables, picking unenthusiastically at the food on their plates.

"I'm Detective Rhonda Pohs," she began, addressing the group for the first time.

"Anyone from this area knows who you are," Skip Carmichael said, getting to his feet. "Your name's been flashed all over the papers for your work as a detective for the county. Are you telling us you're here to investigate Pete's death?"

"I'm here to investigate Mr. Potter's murder. For now, I have to ask that none of you leave. We'll be talking to all of you and recording your interviews. At this point everyone is a suspect."

Concerned murmurs circulated through the men and women who were gathered for what started as a weekend of fun and turned into a weekend of horrors.

"You can't possibly mean 'all' of us," a woman asked, her voice carrying a noticeable southern drawl. "I'm sure none of the women would be involved in anything like this."

Rhonda couldn't help remembering the case involving the cheerleader last fall. Considering the outcome of that case, she didn't put anything past anyone, man, or woman, when murder was involved.

"Depending on the circumstances, everyone is a suspect. As long as you have nothing to hide, this process should be relatively painless. We will be speaking to everyone and recording what you tell us. Whatever you remember, no matter how inconsequential you might think it is, the information could be important in our investigation."

Leaving the shell-shocked classmates to contemplate what she just said, Rhonda followed Phil to the building where the interviews would be taking place. Once inside, she met Brandon Hayes, Jackson's son. He showed her around the studio with all the pride of a new father showing off his first son.

"I'm just getting started," he said, as he pointed out the various pieces of equipment. "I'm hoping to be able to establish my own recording company. There are so many good groups around here. I think it could be very profitable. I've shown your forensics team how to work the equipment, but if you have any problems or questions, I'll be up at the house. Also, for your convenience, there are two recording booths. With the amount of people here, you and your partner can both have private areas for your interviews."

Rhonda looked over the list of the classmates attending this unorthodox reunion. Whoever made it up did their homework well. Each classmate was listed with a complete biography, spanning from their high school days to the present, including married and maiden names for each of the girls.

Not sure whether the list was written in order of the people returning their RSVP letters or by importance in the class, Rhonda started at the beginning, giving Martin the second half of the list to interview. She also gave copies of both lists to Phil so he could send his classmates in to be interviewed in order.

With the IT people in place, Rhonda looked at the list of names in front of her. Earlier she'd asked Phil about the classmates in attendance tonight. Counting himself and Pete Potter there were thirty, with more due to arrive tomorrow.

Considering half the list was fourteen, she knew it could be a long weekend. Nodding to Phil, he ushered in the first of the classmates to be questioned.

According to her list, she would be interviewing Christine Wilson. She could hardly believe her eyes when she noticed Christine listed as captain of the football team.

"Do I have this right?" she asked the tall blond model who seated herself across the table from Rhonda.

Christine smiled. "I know it's confusing. When I was in college, I realized I felt more like a woman than a man. It took a lot of work and surgery, but I'm now *all* woman. In New York, I'm the most sought after mature female model in the business."

As was her usual habit, Rhonda jotted notes furiously. "What was your connection to Mr. Potter?"

"In high school, he was the quarterback, but I was the captain of the team. We always had a rivalry going on between us. I recognized him as soon as I got here tonight. He's still the same bastard he was in high school. I couldn't believe it when he put the make on me. When I turned him down, he looked like he wanted to cry."

Rhonda hardly knew what to say and for a moment sat as though stunned. "I have to ask. Did you have any reason to kill Pete?"

Christine batted her eyes as though attempting to flirt. "Would I kill poor old Pete? Why not? Then again, why should I bother? I have more important things to worry about. As far as I'm concerned Pete Potter was a piss ant in high school and nothing about him has changed in the past twenty-five years. My only regret is he was already missing when I shocked the shit out of all these hicks by telling them I'm a woman now."

Rhonda thanked Christine and checked with the IT guys, who assured her they'd everything recorded.

In direct contrast to Christine, came Mike Krumpy. The past twenty-five years hadn't been kind to Mike. He was a big guy. If she were any judge, Mike had to carry at least three hundred pounds and was balding.

"This business is a crock of shit," Mike said as soon as he seated himself across from Rhonda. "Who'd want to do in Pete? He was one of the good guys."

"Why do you say that?"

"I had two things going for me in high school. The first was I managed to be elected class president and the other was my friendship with Pete. I tried college and dropped out after the first semester. With all my friends making it in school, I felt like an outcast."

"So, what did you do?" Rhonda asked.

"I came back here with my tail between my legs. The first person I ran into was Pete. He was going to the local tech school. You know, getting his generals out of the way before deciding what college to go to. His mom insisted on having me come over for supper that night. By the time I got there his dad had already made arrangements for me to start working for the city. I've had a good job ever since, if you call hauling trash five days a week good. The work is hard, but the money is great and so is the pension. Without Pete and his dad, it's hard telling what would have happened to me."

Mike left the studio, leaving Rhonda completely confused. To hear Christine talk, Pete was a total prick. Listening to Mike, he was a guardian angel. She knew she'd find the real Pete Potter somewhere in the middle. Just where, she wasn't sure.

"Both ends of the spectrum, right?" Phil said once Mike left.

"How did you know? Were you listening at the door?"

"Hardly. I went to school with these guys. Look Rhonda, I know what Pete was from the outside looking in. When we were in school, I would have given anything to be one of the jocks."

Rhonda smiled at Phil's comment. "Are you telling me you were one of the nerds?"

"I was in the middle. You know, the totally average kid in class. Before you ask, I didn't murder Phil. To be truthful, I didn't even want to come tonight, but Judy insisted since it was our twenty-fifth reunion and we are moving to Madison in a couple of weeks, I had to come. High school wasn't my most shining moment. The jocks couldn't see me for dirt, the popular guys were too busy romancing the girls to give me the time of day and the nerds were studying all the time to make the top grades. I was just eking by with my 'c' average."

"So, who did you hang out with?" Rhonda inquired.

"My best friend was Jack Palmer. We were both middle of the road students. We were the kids who skipped school and got caught smoking cigarettes behind the gym."

"Is he coming to the reunion?" Rhonda asked.

Phil's eyes filled with tears. "I wish he could be here. He was killed in an accident on the Interstate three years after we graduated. I knew I was too drunk to drive, so I decided to call my folks for a ride home. Jack told me I was a wimp, and he was going back to Madison to see his girlfriend. That was the last time I saw him. After the accident I decided to change my major and go into law enforcement. I guess I thought I could do something to keep kids from drinking and driving."

"Where were you going to school?"

"I was studying to be a heating and air conditioning tech out at Blackhawk Tech. That was about the time they put in the law enforcement program. I had enough credits from all the preliminary work I'd done so I talked to them and the rest, as they say, is history."

Rhonda felt sorry for her former partner. She'd never known any of his reasons for becoming a cop.

Unfortunately, like so many others, it took a tragedy for him to change the direction his life would eventually take.

"Enough about me," Phil finally said. "Let's see who's next on your list."

Rhonda waited for the next person to come in to be interviewed. Half expecting another guy, she was pleasantly surprised to see a beautiful middle-aged brunette come in to sit across from her.

"I do like the idea of a woman invading a man's world," she said, once she made herself comfortable in the folding chair across the table from Rhonda. "I'm Debbie, I was the head cheerleader in high school."

Rhonda glanced at her notes. "Oh yes, Debbie Collins Dumont."

"I hate to correct you, Detective, but you'd better get the name right. It's Debbie Collins Harrison Witt Dumont. Of course, the late Mr. Dumont is the reason I came tonight."

Rhonda was interested in how being a widow prompted Debbie to come back for the reunion. Before she could ask the question, Debbie continued.

"I got the invitation just before hubby number three passed on. He told me not to grieve too long for him, since he was ready to die and go home to be with the Lord. He also said he wanted me to come back home and find my roots. Of course, with my inheritance, the travel costs were of no concern to me. I wanted to see how everyone else turned out. After this weekend, they can kiss my ass."

Although Rhonda found Debbie interesting, she needed to know where she stood on the subject of Pete and his murder. "Did you and Pete have a history?"

"History? Now that's an interesting way to put it. Good old Pete thought he was God's great gift to not only the football team but also every girl who crossed his path. To be honest, I was thrilled when he asked me to go to the homecoming dance with him during our senior year. I was pretty naïve back then, but I knew enough not to go parking with him out at the lake. After that he told everyone I was like all the other cheerleaders, an airhead."

Debbie paused, as though reliving a painful memory. Actual tears glistened in her hazel eyes. "I showed them. In college, I was not only on the dean's list, but I was also the head cheerleader in my senior year. After graduation, I packed my bags and headed for Dallas, Texas. It didn't take long for me to land a job with the Dallas Cowboys. It was a good gig for me. That's how I met my first husband, Bob Harrison. He took me to Los Angeles. Of course that was the beginning of the end for us, since his mistress lived in one of the suburbs. I guess my mom must have said something to Pete about the divorce because it didn't take him long to just happen to be in Los Angeles on business."

"He came out looking for you?"

Debbie nodded. "What he didn't know was I'd already met hubby number two. Gary Witt was a high roller in Las Vegas. He worked in the city and went to Vegas every weekend. Bob left me with a good settlement and Gary increased my wealth when he took off with a showgirl. When Pete showed up, Gary and I were becoming an item. I didn't have time for Pete and he resented it. After Gary left, I met Johnny. I knew this one was for life. I loved that man and was devastated when he got cancer. I took care of him for the last two years of his life. I would have cared for him forever if he'd asked."

Rhonda ached for Debbie. It was evident her body along with her looks had gotten her many things in life. Unfortunately, the one thing she wanted the most, her life with husband number three, was taken from her.

"After you first saw Pete tonight, did you see him again?"

"I didn't know how anyone could have missed him. He was hitting on every female here including classmates, spouses of classmates and our former class advisor. I wouldn't be surprised if he even tried something with one of Jackson's cows. That's how horny he was. If I were a guy and saw him going after my wife, I'd deck him. I know before his health failed Johnny would have done just that."

Rhonda thanked Debbie and watched as she left the room. The interviews with the first three classmates had taken her an hour and a half. At this rate, she'd be here most of the night. With her list containing fourteen names, and each preliminary interview taking a minimum of a half an hour, she was looking at over five and a half hours to complete this phase of the investigation. She glanced at her watch and realized it was already after eight in the evening.

She got up and stretched. Seeing that Martin was just dismissing the classmate he'd been interviewing, she waited until he was alone to see how he thought the process was going. "How many people have you interviewed?"

"Only two," he replied. "At this rate…"

He rolled his eyes at the enormity of the task.

"I know what you mean. I think we need to talk to Phil and see how long these people plan to stay in the area."

"Do you think he'll cooperate with us? I mean, he is one of the suspects here."

Rhonda bit back a sharp answer. Couldn't Martin see how Phil was helping in setting up the people to come in for interviews? She had to remember this was Martin's first murder case and he had to be jittery.

"I have no qualms about talking to Phil. We were partners for quite a while. He'll be able to tell us if we can depend on the classmates staying here to be interviewed throughout the weekend."

"Slow going, isn't it?"

Rhonda turned at the sound of Phil's voice. "It certainly is. I've only talked to three people in the past hour and a half. Martins only interviewed two of your friends. At this rate, we're going to be here all night."

"While you were busy in here, I talked to everyone, and we've all agreed to stay out here for the entire weekend. There are more people coming tomorrow, but you won't have to consider any of them. We decided to carry on with the reunion as planned. Everything is going to be taking place at the farm, so you'll have a chance to talk to your entire list of suspects, just not all tonight."

"Where are all these people staying?" Martin asked. "If they're at hotels, we could lose contact with them."

Phil shook his head. "This has been well planned. Those of us who either own or rented campers and tents are already at our campsites. Jackson has also opened his home and brought in campers and motorhomes from his friends to accommodate everyone else. The classmates who don't want to camp or stay with Jackson are coming in tomorrow."

"I know the two of you want to stay out here, so Jackson's son has asked if Martin would like to bunk in with him and his wife. I said I'd find out and let him know. As for you Rhonda, Judy has already called Mark and he's packing you a bag. We have plenty of room in our camper for the two of you to join us. That way you won't be up all night doing the investigation. It's best if you get some rest. I'm afraid this is going to turn out to be a long process of elimination. Of course, with the best detective we have investigating it, I have no doubts about it being solved."

Phil's words of assurance put Rhonda's mind at ease. She knew Martin was still skeptical, but he was green and still learning the ropes. "We'll do a couple more interviews tonight and get back to it tomorrow morning. I certainly don't want to wreck a good hangover for you and your classmates."

Phil laughed. "Who do you want to see next?"

Martin gave Phil the names of two classmates and Rhonda did the same. The next two names on her list were Tom Coats, the boy most likely to succeed and Suellen Marsh Neuhouse, the girl most likely to succeed.

Rhonda watched the door and was surprised to see Tom Coats enter the room. Over the years she'd heard stories, mostly from her neighbor, Tom's sister, Eileen. From what she heard; Tom had achieved his goal of making a million by the age of thirty. He must have figured he was set for life, but he'd blown through all of it by the time of his thirty-fifth birthday.

"Hi Tom," Rhonda said when he seated himself across from her.

"Eileen told me you were a cop. From what I hear you're damn good at it, too. I just never expected to be sitting across a table from you as a suspect in a murder."

"You have to know everyone here is suspect, even Phil. What do you know about Pete's murder?"

Tom's brow wrinkled as if deep in thought. "I'm sure you know all the stories about me. I've been living out in San Francisco for the past seven years. The weather is more conducive to being homeless. I owe Pete a lot. He was on vacation there a couple of years ago. After that he kept in touch with me through the mission where I get at least one meal a day and if I'm lucky a bed to sleep in at night. Imagine my surprise when he sent me tickets to come out here for this weekend. He met me at the train station in Columbus on Wednesday and took me shopping for clothes. I was flabbergasted when he had a job interview set up for me. I start work on Monday, and he said I could stay at his place until I could get back on my feet again. Guess that won't work out now."

"Do you have any idea who could have killed Pete?"

"I know it wasn't me. Why would I kill the goose that laid the golden eggs? I owe that man more than I can ever hope to be able to repay. I've been lost for a long time and Pete was the only one of my old friends who ever gave a damn. My family tried to help, but their timing wasn't good. Eileen just lost her job and Mom and Dad weren't having an easy time either. I just couldn't take money from them when I knew they were all struggling."

Rhonda turned to the last page of her legal pad where she was keeping score on the pros and cons about Pete Potter. Under the good guy heading she now had two hash marks and under the dirty dog heading were another two marks. It was still early in the investigation and the sides were already forming. She wondered how many more former classmates would step forward to sing Pete's praises.

Before Rhonda could come to any decisions, Suellen Marsh Neuhouse came in to see her. She recognized Suellen immediately. She should; over the years Suellen had been in enough little theater productions and was known to just about everyone in town. Rather than being shapely, she was a bit on the chunky side, making her a perfect character actress. Others could play the lead in the plays while Suellen brought the comic relief.

"I should say it's good to see you, Rhonda, but these aren't the best of circumstances, are they?"

"Not really. I have to ask; do you know anything about Pete's murder?"

Suellen shook her head and Rhonda noticed a hint of tears in her eyes. "Don't get me wrong, Pete and I got along, but they didn't call him Sneaky Pete for nothing. I'm going to miss him trying to cop a feel whenever we're together. He wasn't so open about it when he was married, but since the divorce I think he was getting desperate."

"What do you mean cop a feel?"

"Come on Rhonda, you're not that naive. After every play there's usually a reception line. When someone you know comes through, they give you a congratulatory hug, only Pete always seemed to be able to do it with one hand so he could feel up my boobs with his free one. They're the only good part of being on the heavy side. I have a good rack, you know, nice and cushy, for anyone who's a boob man. At least that's what my husband says."

Rhonda tried not to smile. As a teenager she wanted to be well endowed, but now, as a detective, she was just as happy with her slender frame.

"If you ask me," Suellen continued, "I'd be looking at the spouses of the female classmates. All of the girls have been fending off Pete ever since we started to develop. Our husbands aren't always as understanding about such things."

Without commenting on what Suellen said, Rhonda added a new heading to her list. Even calling the victim Sneaky Pete, Suellen didn't hate or love the man. She was more or less neutral where Pete was concerned. He was little more than an annoying lifelong friend.

"Time to call it a night," Phil said, as he came into the studio where Rhonda was conducting interviews.

Rhonda stood and stretched. "This is turning out to be one hell of an investigation. I didn't know you went to school with such a crazy bunch of characters. Right now, I'd just like to get to know the real Pete Potter."

"That might be harder than you think. I doubt if any of us ever knew what he was like."

"I don't like the sound of your comment. Someone must have known the man. What about his ex-wife?"

"You can scratch that one. She'll probably be celebrating as soon as she hears about this."

Rhonda rolled her eyes. The woman couldn't possibly be that hard hearted, could she?

"So, when are you going to be interviewing me?" Phil asked, breaking the silence of the past few seconds.

"How about never? I can't be objective about you and Martin can. I don't even know if Mark and I should be staying in your camper."

"Not to worry. I know better than to try and pick your brain. To be truthful, I was the first one Martin interviewed. As much as I want in on this investigation, I know it's impossible. Not only am I a suspect, but I'm no longer with the county. Even with my new position, I won't be starting there until after Labor Day. I guess you could say I'm in between assignments. As for staying in the camper, Judy insisted on having Mark bring out your tent and she's banished me out there. She said you could share the bedroom of the motor home with her and if I want to do any late-night drinking or reminiscing, I won't bother you when I come back. Mark was a good sport about it and volunteered to stay out there with me."

Rhonda thought about the difference between Phil and her current partner. She doubted Martin would be so considerate of her feelings in a situation like this one. She remembered going to Alabama with Phil while working on the Adkins case. The small-town police chief they met down there was certain the two of them were sleeping together. Phil set things straight, saying he had no desire to have an affair or do anything to make his partner uncomfortable.

Packing her legal pad in her briefcase, Rhonda followed Phil to the area set aside for the campgrounds. Having seen the motor home Phil purchased a couple of years earlier, she wasn't surprised at the luxury it afforded. To be truthful, she could have stayed in the tent with her husband, but Phil insisted on willingly giving up his bed so she could rest comfortably. Considering the summer heat, she would certainly appreciate the air conditioning the unit afforded.

"I'm surprised Phil gave up this bed," Rhonda said, once she got out of her work clothes and into her nightshirt.

"I'm not," Judy replied. "He knows how important a good night's sleep is when he's on a case. Besides, I know he doesn't expect to do much sleeping this weekend. He's made a lot of noise about not coming, but I know he's looking forward to spending time with some of the guys from out of town. He likes to come off as not caring, but there are a few people who went to school with him from kindergarten to high school graduation. If the truth were known, they were a fairly close-knit group. Of course, with all the drinking going on, someone might let something slip that could be of help to you."

Rhonda nodded. Judy was still doing a few things around the motor home. She insisted Rhonda should go to bed and she'd be along as soon as she finished straightening up.

Outside the door to the bedroom, Rhonda could hear Mark and Phil talking about going back out to join everyone at the bonfire. Knowing Mark, he would fit in well. He seemed to get along with everyone.

Instead of listening further, Rhonda's mind spun out of control with the information she'd gleaned from Phil's classmates tonight. Although she'd already seen five of the people on her list, there were still nine more to talk to, without mentioning spouses.

The thought of spouses brought to mind Suellen's comment. It wasn't only the husbands of the female classmates, but she couldn't forget the wives of the men. They were all unknown factors. Anyone could snap, and with Pete Potter's track record, it wouldn't take much to put the wrong person over the edge.

Chapter Three

Rhonda awoke to the smell of coffee. She reached over for Mark then remembered she was in Phil's camper and had spent the night with Judy while Mark and Phil went to the bonfire and slept in the tent outside.

As soon as she opened the door between the bedroom and kitchen of the unit, she saw Judy making coffee. "Good morning," Rhonda said.

"I hope I didn't wake you," Judy replied.

"Hardly. I've got too much on my mind to sleep late. Phil's lucked out on this one. At least he can get some rest."

Judy rolled her eyes. "It's more like he passed out. I don't know how late it was when he got back here with Mark last night, but knowing that bunch, it couldn't have been early. I heard them come back to the tent. I should have checked out the clock, but I didn't want to know what time it was. Even though they were trying to be quiet, they were both in the bag, so to speak. I think he had every intention of helping you out, but I know these guys, I'm sure they drank more than one toast to good old Pete."

While Judy finished up in the kitchen, Rhonda took her clothes into the bathroom to get ready for the coming day. By the time she cleaned up, Judy sat out at the picnic table with two cups of coffee.

"This certainly wasn't the weekend any of us planned," Judy said, pushing one of the cups toward Rhonda.

"What do you know about Pete?" Rhonda asked, after tasting the coffee.

"I was a year behind this class. Pete always had a reputation. How much of it was true is anyone's guess. He's the kind of guy you either love or hate. There's no middle ground. Phil and I live far enough away we didn't come in contact with him, but we still heard the rumors, especially when Donna divorced him."

"I wouldn't say on the other side of the county is that far away."

"With this bunch it is. Most of these guys still live in town and have to contend with Pete on a regular basis. He's their insurance man and this is a small town. The only time we come back here is to either see my folks or to go out to supper."

Rhonda nodded. She understood what Judy was saying. "You said Donna divorced Pete. Did she catch him in one of his affairs?"

Judy laughed. "Good heavens no. Pete talked a good game, but when it came to the follow through, he couldn't hold a candle to Donna. At one time or another she screwed every guy in town. She finally left him for Skip Carmichael, but that didn't last either. She was in my class and the last I heard she moved to Portland with some guy none of us ever heard about before."

"It sounds like they deserved each other."

"They did. I talked to Janet Krumpy last night and she said she was going to call Donna. They were good friends in school. If she shows up, you're in for a real treat. She was a beauty in high school and still was at our last reunion. There was more than one guy wanting to get in her pants even twenty years after graduation."

Rhonda marveled about the sexual exploits in this small town. Finishing her coffee she saw Martin coming toward her. "Are you ready to talk to more of these classmates?" she asked when Judy went in to get them each another cup of coffee.

"Hardly. I can't believe Sheriff Cantwell is going along with us staying out here in the middle of nowhere. Everyone I've talked to is little more than a hick. They have no idea why Mr. Potter was killed. They're more interested in bragging about his exploits and getting drunk."

Rhonda shook her head. When she first met Martin, he told her he'd come from Milwaukee because of the offer of going from beat cop to detective. Working for a county force rather than one in the city, she was certain he was experiencing the first of many culture shocks this job would provide. Rather than comment on his first encounter with rural life, she decided to keep their conversation professional. "What do you think their feelings about Pete are?"

"I have the impression the late Mr. Potter was one of those guys you love to hate."

They continued to compare notes from the interviews of the previous evening until someone came over to tell them the buffet breakfast was being served at the main house.

Sitting with Martin, she wished she could be privy to the conversations of the classmates. Unfortunately, considering the circumstances, it was impossible.

"Is this a private party or can anyone join in?" Phil asked, as he sat down at their table.

Rhonda saw the look of disgust on Martin's face.

"Should you be talking to us?" Martin snapped.

"Phil's not the enemy here," Rhonda admonished.

"Isn't he a suspect?"

"Technically, yes, but we were partners long enough I'm certain he's one of the good guys."

"Thanks Rhonda," Phil said with a wink. "I was with my buddies last night and there was a lot of talk about the murder. Last night, after it happened, everyone was in shock and the fact I was a cop made them a little leery of talking to me about it. Of course, after a few drinks, they all loosened up."

"So, what did you learn?"

"Most of the guys were pissed off about the way Pete was coming on to their wives, even though it was nothing unexpected. Christine even joined us. It's hard to think of her as a woman, but she put a whole new twist on things."

"She told me Pete tried to put the moves on her," Rhonda said. "What did she tell you?"

Phil laughed. "Talk about one hacked off lady. She said he tried to feel up her boobs and suggested they find some secluded spot where they could get it on. After she turned him down, he went on to new conquests."

"Sounds like the lady still has balls," Martin remarked, before he realized what he just said.

"You've got her pegged all right," Phil agreed. "She used to have balls. According to her, she had everything taken off about five years ago. Of course, I didn't check it out. I don't want to know. As for good old Pete, from what I heard, he was off to try and make another conquest before the evening was over. Everyone said he must have hit on the wrong woman. I tend to agree with them."

Rhonda wished she had this conversation on tape, but knew Phil's observations were just that, observations. He was trying to help, but these were the people he'd known all his life. She knew he was a good cop, but would he draw the line at incriminating his friends?

~ * ~

With the perfect weather, the last place Rhonda wanted to be on a Saturday was in the farm's recording studio doing interviews. She glanced at her list and noticed the next name was Evan-Skip-Carmichael. Just reading the name reminded her about what Judy said over coffee this morning. This was the man who prompted Donna's divorce from Pete.

Skip certainly wasn't exactly what Rhonda expected. Even seeing Pete's body last night, Rhonda knew this man couldn't hold a candle to the corpse. She wondered why Donna left her husband for this guy.

"I know what you're thinking," Skip said once he sat down across from Rhonda.

"Oh, really?" she replied. "What would that be?"

"I'm sure you heard about Pete's wife, Donna, and me. In high school, I was a real runt. As much as I wanted to play football, all I could do was be the waterboy. I took a lot of ribbing about that."

Rhonda stared at the man in front of her. At this point in time, she'd certainly never call him a runt. He stood well over six feet tall and weighed at least two hundred and fifty pounds with hardly an ounce of fat anywhere on his body.

"Why would you say such a thing?"

"Because when I moved back here, Pete wouldn't let me forget I'd been too scrawny to play football in high school. I was pretty good in college but of course I went through a growth spurt the summer after our senior year."

"What happened between you and Donna Potter?"

Skip took a deep breath. "When Donna first came on to me, I thought I'd died and gone to heaven. She led me on saying we'd get married as soon as she got her divorce. Like a fool, I started planning for *our* future. In reality, she was using me as an easy way out of a bad situation. They only had one kid and that was the reason they got married in the first place. When Chad started college, Donna decided she didn't want to be married to Pete anymore."

"What happened when the divorce was final?"

"I found out what Pete went through for the nineteen years of their marriage. Every time I turned around, I was hearing rumors about Donna and another guy. I was smart enough to get out when I did. We had great sex, but it didn't last. I can only imagine what Pete went through with all her affairs. It's no wonder he was out there being an old tomcat."

"Did you talk to Pete about it?"

"Hell no. Pete and I went to school together and screwed the same woman, but we didn't have anything else in common. He had his big insurance business and I'm working in a factory. We didn't travel in the same circles."

After Skip left the room, Rhonda put a second hash mark in the *I really don't give a damn* column.

Rhonda checked her list to see which classmate would be in next. The words 'class clown' following the name John Mallory were completely unexpected, leaving her to wonder what she should expect. The man who came in looked distinguished even in casual clothing. "Won't you have a seat, Mr. Mallory?"

"It's Dr. Mallory and I certainly don't know why I'm here. I'm a respected dentist in LaCrosse. I'm beginning to think I made a bad decision to come back and see all these jerks again."

"Is this the first reunion you've attended?"

"You guessed it. I've got a good dental practice. It seems like I've always been out of the country when these things are planned. I'm usually in Bogotá working at a free clinic when they have the reunions. It just so happens I went early this year since my wife insisted, we needed to come here."

"Did you get to talk to Pete before he was killed?"

"If you can call it that. He was bragging about his prowess on the football team. I couldn't get a word in edgewise. That's when he caught a glimpse of my wife. He was actually drooling over her, so I found someone else to talk to and took her with me. Nothing against Pete, but at forty-three you'd think he'd have grown up."

"Do you have any idea who killed him?"

"You can probably put the name of every guy here in a hat and choose one. Pete was an annoying little gnat. He pissed me off coming on to my wife, but I didn't think it was worth my time to say anything to him about it. I tolerated him in high school. I figured I could overlook his behavior for a weekend."

"Only now you're locked into this case for more than the weekend. Like everyone else here last night, you're a suspect. I just hope we find out who the murderer is soon, so the rest of you can get on with your lives and forget this nightmare ever happened."

Dr. Mallory nodded his head. "I hear what you're saying. I don't understand any of what has happened since we got here. I think everyone thought I'd be the same clown I was in high school. What they didn't know was that playing the fool was my way of coping. My home life sucked. My dad was a workaholic. When he did come home it was to complain about everything and dole out punishment to us kids. Mom was a wimp, and her way of coping was to tell us we'd be punished when our dad got home. After that she'd go back to her hidden stash and get happily sloshed. Even though my grades were good, if I got anything below a B the old man would go ballistic. I tried to be friends with everyone in our class so that I could spend nights at their houses when I knew my dad was on the warpath."

"Were you friends with everyone?"

"At the time I thought so, but you have to know just because we were in the same class, we weren't bosom buddies, lifelong friends. Just like in life, there were people you tolerated and some you downright hated. Pete was one of those I tolerated. His mother was always nice to me and let me spend the night. She was a good friend to my mother, and I think she understood what my home life was like. Even so, Pete was a hard guy to get close to. I wasn't into sports like he was and therefore not at the top of his list of friends. We were more like acquaintances."

Rhonda looked over her notes for several minutes after John left. In reality, she decided he was the most forthcoming of any of the classmates she'd interviewed so far. What he said about the façade he put up as a kid made a lot of sense. In thinking about the kids she went to high school with, she realized how little she knew of any of their lives away from school. Only several years after graduation did some of those secret lives come to light. Also thinking about her classmates, she realized there were some she was extremely close to, others she couldn't stand to be around and the remainder made up the category John called acquaintances.

"Are you ready for me?" a woman asked, breaking into Rhonda's thoughts.

She looked up. "Of course, let's see, you're Kathy Gransee White."

"Oh no, I'm Kandice Kane Whitaker. Kathy had to go to the bus stop to pick up her daughter. She'll be back this afternoon, so she asked me if I'd mind taking her place. I hope that's all right. I was also wondering if you would mind if my husband came in with me."

Rhonda looked past the woman standing in front of her to see a man, probably four to five years older than his wife, standing at the door. "Is there any reason why you want your husband with you?"

"I'm just very nervous about all of this. I mean my latest cookbook just came out and I wouldn't want any bad publicity to spoil its reception. Jack is more than my husband, he's also my publicist."

Rhonda scanned the list of classmates until she came across the name of Kandice Kane Whitaker. The fact the woman had been named the Betty Crocker Homemaker Award winner twenty-five years ago made the mention of a new cookbook being released make some sort of sense. "I don't see any reason why he can't be with you. What kind of a relationship did you have with Pete?"

Kandice seated herself across from Rhonda and held tightly to her husband's hand. "In high school, Pete always made fun of me because I was always cooking and baking. I had to since my mother worked full time after my father passed away. I pretty much kept our house running smoothly. I was pleased when I won the award, but Pete laughed at it and called it a stupid award. Of course, what more could you expect from one of the top jocks in the school?"

"So, you weren't friends?"

"Not in school, but he changed his tune when my first cookbook came out. He came to my first signing and bought several copies. When I met Jack and got married, Pete told him he was lucky to get such a good cook for a wife. We got all of our insurance from Pete and when I ran for Mrs. Wisconsin, he insisted on being one of my backers. He was the one who talked me into writing this new book. I promised him the first copy and was going to give it to him tonight." She dabbed at her eyes with a tissue and seemed to be too choked up to say anything more.

"What my wife is trying to say," Jack said, "is that we worked well professionally with Pete. He was our agent and I trusted him with all of our insurance needs. We know all about his reputation as well as that of his ex-wife, but you can't always tell the contents of a book by its cover. To the world he was a cheating bastard, but to us he was a good friend. We'll miss him."

With this final interview of the morning finished, Rhonda thought about Jack's statement. It was evident he was used to giving press releases and saying exactly what anyone thought he should say. She wondered how much stock she could put into their statements.

"I'm supposed to come and get you for lunch," Mark said as he entered the studio.

"Is it that late already? I mean I've only interviewed three classmates."

"Well, get ready for a surprise when you come out for lunch. Last night there were only about thirty classmates here. This morning the number has almost doubled. Phil told me not everyone could get out here for the entire weekend, so they were coming out for today's activities only, you know, make an entire day out of it."

Rhonda groaned. She'd only made it through eight of the fourteen classmates on her list, the thought of even more people wandering around and compromising her investigation defeated her.

"Kandice, the gal who just left here with her husband, said Kathy Gransee White left to pick up her daughter. Who leaves their class reunion to pick up their kid? What I want to know is why the kid is here in the first place?"

"I think we need to talk about this. I was with Phil when Kathy came to him about her daughter, Iris. It seems in high school Pete got Kathy

29

pregnant. She didn't tell anyone about it and went away right after graduation. Iris is Pete's daughter. Kathy called her last night to tell her about the murder and she called her mother today to say she wanted to come out. I didn't get the whole story, but somehow Pete found out about Iris when she was fourteen. A couple of years ago he came to New York to meet her. I guess it wasn't a pretty scene and Kathy got a restraining order against him. I don't know how the daughter feels about it, but I'm sure we'll find out when they get back from the bus depot."

Rhonda realized Mark made sense. It was already noon, and she could certainly use a break. This would prove to be a long afternoon, with interviews lasting far into the evening. In the usual cases she investigated, the suspects were in the area. This time many of those under suspicion would be leaving on Sunday for the four corners of the country. Whatever questions she needed answers to would have to be asked in the next thirty-six hours or go unanswered.

Chapter Four

The amount of people crowding into the pole shed to partake of the buffet lunch was overwhelming. It appeared the entire class had decided to return for their twenty-fifth celebration.

Among the middle-aged classmates reuniting and catching up on old friends, while learning about and coping with Pete's murder, were two young people who didn't seem to belong. Rhonda glanced at Mark, hoping he could shed some light on the identities of the twenty something intruders.

"I assume the girl with Kathy White must be her daughter Iris Gransee. The woman with the young man is a stranger, though. If I don't miss my guess, that's Chad Potter and his mother, Donna."

Rhonda agreed and made a note to interview both of the women who'd been, at one time, involved with Pete Potter, as well as the grown children representing the product of both unions.

"How are things going?" Phil asked, as he guided her to the buffet line.

"You know I can't tell you much," Rhonda replied. "This is a rough case. You have to know there was very little gray area when it came to Mr. Potter. You either loved him, hated him, or really didn't give a damn."

Phil laughed at her observation. "Guess I fall into the last category. If I know you, you're keeping track. Do you think Martin is doing the same with the people he's interviewing?"

Rhonda nodded. "We compared notes this morning. I told him how I was doing things and I think it shocked him to realize he was doing his investigation in the same way. We both agreed about the perception of Mr. Potter by his classmates."

Rhonda picked up a Styrofoam plate, ending her conversation with Phil, who headed down to the opposite side of the table. After filling her plate, she looked for a place to sit. Phil was already seated with several of his friends. Not wanting to intrude, she went to where Judy sat with some of the wives.

"I saved you a seat," Judy said, scooting over on the bench of the picnic table where they were sitting. "This is Alison Krumpy, Julia Mallory, Cynthia Grant, Malinda Carpenter and Jasmine Pooler," she continued, as she made the necessary introductions.

Rhonda recognized several of the names, matching them with the ones on her list. Only the name of Pooler didn't sound at all familiar.

"If nothing else, this has been one hell of a reunion," Cynthia observed. "What happened to Pete last night was horrible, but if I know my husband, he's already trying out how to work this into the plot of his next book." "Book?" Rhonda questioned.

"Of course, you wouldn't know," Cynthia replied. "Marshall was the editor of the school newspaper in his senior year. In college he studied journalism and creative writing. After graduation, he worked on the newspaper just to put food on our table until he quit to write his novels on a full-time basis."

"Is he successful?" Julie asked.

"As successful as any mid-list author can be. He's no James Patterson, but he thinks he is. His books don't pay the bills, but they give him satisfaction. Thank goodness I have a good job and he has an inheritance from his grandmother. At least I don't have to depend on the royalties to keep us out of the poor house."

"Well, at least, your husband is getting something out of this nightmare," Julie commented. "I only saw Pete for a couple of minutes last night, but I could tell John wasn't happy to see him. I've been around a lot of guys, but Pete was the only one I ever felt really uncomfortable being in his company. To be truthful, I felt like I'd been raped just by the way he looked at me. I caught hell from John last night because I insisted he come to this reunion. I can't imagine I'll live this one down anytime in the near future."

Rhonda held her tongue. She was learning far more about the classmates from the spouses than she ever would have through the interviews. Red flags went up just listening to Julie Mallory. It was evident from her earlier interview with the woman's husband that he blamed her for thinking they should come this weekend. Listening to her now, Rhonda saw the charismatic dentist as someone with a violent temper who could become an abuser in the blink of an eye. Could he become abusive to the point of murder? It was only one of several scenarios she knew would play out over the course of the weekend.

"Well, I'm relieved my husband had to work last night," Jasmine Pooler said. "I can't imagine being here when they found Pete's body. Dan and Pete were close. He's taking this really hard."

"How do you feel about Pete?" Rhonda finally asked.

"You know how it is with your husband's friends. I can't say I always agree with his choices. I tried to get close to Donna, but we were so different, I just couldn't warm up to her. After the divorce, Pete and Dan got together for lunch while I was at work. I certainly didn't care since the man always made me nervous."

"Did he ever come on to you?" Rhonda questioned, wishing she had a recorder going for this lunchtime conversation.

"He tried, but I made it perfectly clear I didn't want any part of it. He came over to the house while Dan was at work and put the moves on me. It was right after Donna left. I kneed him as hard as I could and said if he ever came back for more, I'd tell Dan what he did. Of course, I told Dan as soon as he got home from work. We made a deal that night. I wouldn't rag on him about his friends, and he'd make sure I never had to be alone with Pete again. It worked. I knew I'd see him this weekend, but I also knew he couldn't get within spitting distance of me. Dan says I had him scared shitless."

Everyone at the table laughed. Even though Rhonda joined them, she silently wished she could be sitting at a table with the male spouses of the classmates. If Jasmine was this upset about Pete's advances, how would the husband of one of the girls who knew Pete twenty-five years ago feel? Hopefully, one of the men sitting with Martin would shed some light in that direction.

~ * ~

Rhonda's afternoon schedule was completely upset when Kathy

Gransee White and her daughter, Iris, requested an interview with her. Another surprise came when Donna and her son, Chad, also asked for a meeting.

Kathy and Iris came in together looking so much alike it wasn't hard to believe they were each sought after actresses.

"Why did you come back for this reunion?" Rhonda asked Kathy once the two women were seated at her table.

"I've lived in fear of coming back here for the last twenty-five years," Kathy began. "I was the star of the senior class play. Pete was the leading man, and we were doing Barefoot in the Park. It was easy to fall for the same lines he said in the play. After the cast party, he took me home and well, one thing led to another, and we ended up in the backseat of his dad's car. Needless to say, nine months later, Iris was born. I honestly didn't think I could ever come back here and face my friends knowing I'd gotten pregnant and had a baby to raise without a father."

"Did anyone from town know about what happened to you?"

"My folks knew and were mortified. They insisted I go to New York and stay with my aunt and uncle until the baby was born. Once there, I carved out a new life for myself and never came back. I think Mom and Dad were secretly relieved. They were happy to come to New York to see us but didn't have to explain my baby and me to the neighbors. The one person I did tell was my best friend, Ginny Martin."

Rhonda made notes furiously as Kathy talked.

"I've been back in the area for the last two weeks. Ginny got married fifteen years ago and moved to Rockford. She called me three weeks ago and told me she'd been diagnosed with pancreatic cancer. She said she didn't think she'd be able to make it to the reunion. I dropped everything and stayed with her until she passed last Monday."

"Were you planning to attend before that?"

Tears filled Kathy's eyes and Rhonda handed her a tissue. "We both were. We decided after twenty-five years we'd come and show everyone here how we turned out. I faced Pete two years ago when he came to New York. I found out he was stalking Iris and confronted him about it. We'd been in contact ten years ago when Iris was hired by a modeling agency for a spread in a national magazine. At the time he wanted to meet her, but I put him off for eight years. I think he was relieved to think I wasn't pressing him to pay child support. I told him I could take him to court and ask for fourteen years of back support but if he left her alone, I wouldn't pressure him for it."

Rhonda looked at Kathy's daughter. "Were you in favor of meeting your biological father?"

Iris met Rhonda's gaze. "I've always known who my father was and to be truthful, when I was a kid, I fantasized about him. He called the magazine and asked about me ten years ago. They called me and I took his information. I was only fourteen, so Mom helped me draft a letter to him, but only after I learned more about the man. I thanked him for giving me life and told him thanks but no thanks on the Daddy Dearest routine. Mom's husband, Alan White, has been my father since I was three and I didn't need Pete Potter."

"Your mother said you met him two years ago. How did that come about?"

"According to him, he takes a vacation every year on the anniversary of his divorce. That year he just happened to come to New York. He told me he was shocked to see me as one of the characters in the play he got tickets for. It all seemed too coincidental to me. For the next three days, he dogged me almost constantly. I finally had to get a restraining order against him. The only good thing to come out of it was I found out I have a brother. I did my research well and made the first contact with Chad."

Rhonda made note of the brother/sister relationship on her pad. "Did you ever meet Chad?"

"I did. Last year I had a couple of weeks off at Christmas. After the holiday, Chad and I made plans to meet in Florida. I'm glad we had that time to get to know each other. We've been in contact ever since. We even got together this summer to celebrate his graduation from college."

"Have you seen each other today?"

"Of course, we have. Mom was picking me up at the bus station. To my surprise, Donna was on the same bus. Both Mom and Chad were waiting for us."

"Didn't you know Donna?"

"Why should I? I've never even met her. I honestly couldn't

understand why Mom and Chad were both meeting the bus. You have to remember I only found my brother a couple of years ago. By that time, both Pete and Donna were out of his life."

Rhonda knew Donna lived in Portland. Was it possible her son stayed in the area? If so, why would Iris say Pete was out of his son's life?

After Kathy and Iris left, Rhonda looked over the pages of notes she'd made during the interview. Iris didn't strike her as a grieving daughter, just as Kathy could be listed in the 'I don't give a damn' column.

It took only moments for Donna and Chad to come in and sit across the table from her. If she expected a grieving widow, she was in for a surprise. Donna was more like the merry widow.

"I knew it was only a matter of time before someone did in my newly departed ex. Who did it, a pissed off husband?"

"That's what we're trying to find out. How long have you been divorced?"

A contented smile crossed Donna's lips. "This year it will be six years since I got rid of that skirt chasing son of a bitch. I only came here to be of comfort to my son."

Rhonda stared at the mother and son. Neither of them looked as though they needed comfort. "Do you live in the area, Chad?" Rhonda asked.

"Not here, exactly. After I graduated from college, I got a job in Appleton."

"How did you hear about your father's murder?"

"Mr. Krumpy used to date my mom. For a while, I thought he was going to be my stepfather. I always liked him. We've kept in contact over the years, even though I rarely talk to my own father."

"I can't believe you stay in contact with that piece of shit. I only dated him to let your father see other men found me attractive. I never thought my own son would turn against me and become close with Mike."

Angry sparks flashed from Chad's eyes as he pushed back his chair. "I'll talk to you later, Detective Pohs, when I can be alone and not have my every word scrutinized by her." He nodded at his mother before storming out of the room.

"Has your relationship with your son always been this tense?"

"I'm afraid so."

"Who got custody of him after the divorce?"

"I did. He lived with Mike and me for a couple of years, but that relationship went to hell in a hand basket. By the time I moved on, Chad was in college. At least Pete had the decency to pay his half of the tuition every year."

"Did you pay your half?"

"Well, I couldn't afford it. Thank goodness Chad got some scholarships and student loans. He still had to work, but my new husband didn't want to be bothered with paying for my adult kid's education. He was capable of getting a job to pay his own way. It made a man out of him."

"I've heard a lot about Pete's affairs," Rhonda said, trying to disguise her distaste for the things Donna said about her son. "I've also heard about yours. Is there any truth to any of it?"

"Hell, yes, there's truth. Pete chased any skirt that crossed his path, but he was far from a great lover. I have a feeling if he really caught one, he'd be like a dog with a car. He wouldn't have known what to do with it. I got sick of him bragging about all the women who wanted a piece from him, so I started doing the same thing. The only problem was having a kid kinda put a crimp in my style, if you get my drift."

"So why come back now?"

"What would it have looked like if I didn't? I mean I wanted nothing to do with Pete, but I didn't want the bastard to go and get himself killed. Since my current husband didn't come with me, I thought I might hook up with someone here and the weekend wouldn't be a total loss. Since Chad and I are Pete's only family, someone has to plan the funeral. I'm sure he's got enough insurance to cover the extravaganza I have in mind."

"Do you have any idea who killed your ex-husband?"

"I wish I did. I'd go and pin a medal on him or her. Whoever it was, they did a favor for every woman within a one-hundred-mile radius."

Rhonda thought Chad left but was surprised to see him return to the chair next to his mother. She also didn't miss the way Chad rolled his eyes in response to his mother's derogatory statement.

"Can I go now?" Donna asked, annoyance sounding in her voice.

"If I have more questions, I'm sure I'll be able to get in touch with you. Just leave the information of where you're staying with Phil Mason."

"Oh, I'll be easy to find. If I can't hook up with someone here, I'll just go to Pete's house. He certainly doesn't need it."

"I doubt that," Chad declared. "I happen to know Dad had the locks changed last year after he had a break in. He made a big deal out of giving me a key."

"Well, you can get me in so why wouldn't I be staying there?"

"Because, Mommy Dearest, I wouldn't feel right about having you go there. I want nothing to do with his house and you have no right to it." He reached into his pocket and produced a business card, scrawled something on the back and handed it to Rhonda. "You can reach me on my cell, Detective."

Donna turned to leave in a huff. When Chad got up to follow her, Rhonda stopped him. "Do you mind staying for a moment to talk to me?"

"I should have known better than to talk to a female cop," Donna spat. "I suppose you'll want to get into my son's pants. If he's anything like his old man, you'll get laid about as soon as I leave this room."

"Mom," Chad exclaimed. "Get your mind out of the gutter. I thank God every day I'm not like either one of my parents." Without saying another word, Donna stormed out of the room.

"I'm sorry for the way my mother, and I use the term lightly, acted," Chad said, as he sat back down across from Rhonda. "I honestly don't know what I can tell you. I haven't even talked to my dad since Christmas."

"Earlier you told me you wanted to talk to me without your mother. What did you want to say?"

Chad ran his tongue over his lips before he answered. "Look Detective, I'm only here because Mr. Krumpy told me I had to be here. As far as I'm concerned, this might as well be one of those senseless murders that take place every day and have nothing to do with me. I wrote off both my parents a long time ago. It helped that my dad paid his share of my tuition, but I still had to work my butt off. I'm no different than anyone else in my class, but I'm sure I was the only graduate whose father showed up with his latest girlfriend and my mom couldn't be bothered to be there."

"Is that enough reason for you to want your dad dead?" Rhonda asked, almost afraid to hear the answer.

"Hardly. It would be different if I really gave a damn, but as far as I'm concerned, Pete was little more than a sperm donor and Donna an incubator. He's always been out sniffing tail and she's been like a bitch in heat. I'm here because I have to be. When I talked to Iris, she said we needed to come. I agreed to do this for her, nothing more."

"Do you know who the beneficiary of your father's estate is?"

"Of course, I do. When the old man came up to give me the key to his house, he told me he just rewrote his will and split everything equally between Iris and me. I told him I didn't want anything to do with it and I was pretty sure Iris would feel the same way. I talked to Iris' mother about it and she agreed with everything I said. Unless he changed the will, I guess we'll have to decide what to do with it."

Rhonda was still trying to get a clear picture of Pete Potter. With everything she'd learned she didn't blame Chad and Iris for not wanting anything to do with the man who fathered them.

"Phil told me to come in and see you."

Rhonda looked up at the woman who entered the room. It was easy to picture her twenty-five years ago. Rhonda had no doubt she'd been a real beauty in her prime. Now it was evident that years of hard living and sun worship had definitely taken its toll. "Won't you have a seat, Mrs…"

"It's Ms. Geri Salazar. I was Geri Arner. You wouldn't know it, but in high school I was the prom queen for our class. I'm probably one of the few people here who could call Pete a friend."

Rhonda made note of the grief sounding in Geri's voice and mirrored in her eyes.

"What can you tell me about Mr. Potter?"

Geri dabbed at her eyes with a tissue from the box Rhonda placed on the table earlier. To her surprise the tears seemed genuine.

"I know what my classmates say about me. I slept with the majority of these guys, but my date for the prom was Pete. That was the first time I made it with him. Unlike Kathy, I was on the pill and didn't get knocked up. I was a fool to let him get away from me."

"What happened between the two of you?"

Geri got quiet as though reliving a memory from the past. "I thought

I wanted to get out of this hick town. The first thing I did was train to be a flight attendant. The first year I was in the air, I met Josh Salazar. To make a long story short, Johnny Cash said it best. We got married in a fever. We lived hard and fast. He had a place in Miami, and I was the trophy wife and spent my days drinking by the pool. When poor old Josh kicked off, I decided to come home."

"What happened to your husband?"

"He was a lot older than me and had a heart attack while we were having wild monkey sex. Needless to say, I didn't have much in common with my neighbors. That's when I sold my house and moved back home. The first guy I ran into was Pete. Donna had just left and so we picked up where we left off. I soon learned Pete wasn't only a good lover, he was also a cross dresser. I kept a complete wardrobe for him at my house and about once a month the two of us would go to Madison bar hopping. He made a damn good woman. We'd have so much fun getting the drunks up there all hot and bothered. When we'd get home, we'd make love until dawn. I'm gonna miss him."

"Did anyone else know about Pete's cross dressing?"

"Not around here. There is quite a community of crossdressers in Madison and Pete told me he'd been meeting with them. I never talked about it to any of our classmates or friends and I'm sure Pete didn't advertise it."

"Do you think this information is enough to get him killed?"

Geri thought for a moment before answering. "These guys want to think they're macho as hell, but I doubt there's a one of them with the balls to do Pete in. If you ask me, I'd be looking at Marcy Allen Olson. He was always on her ass."

"What do you mean?"

"She was our class valedictorian. Word was she did his homework to keep him on the team. Now she's some hard ass lawyer. From what I hear, she represented Donna in the divorce and took Pete for everything but the house and the clothes on his back. I remember Pete telling me it was a good thing Marcy had brass balls, because her husband, Dave, was always such a wiener."

Once Geri left the room, Rhonda shook her head in dismay. This was going to be one very difficult case to solve. It was already late on Saturday night, and she still had three classmates to interview. It would do no good to do anything further tonight. These people were here to party and even Pete Potter's horrific murder wasn't going to stop them.

She scanned the last three names on the list and noted Marcy and David Olson as well as Tony Carpenter lived in the area. Before she went back home tonight, she would talk to all three of them and make appointments to meet with them at the office.

"Are you ready to go home?" Mark asked when she finally made her way back to Phil and Judy's campsite.

"More than ready," Rhonda replied. "I plan to take a hot bath and sleep straight through until Monday."

"I'm with you there," Martin said, when he joined them. "I didn't know there could be so many different opinions of one man. I talked to the people who taped the interviews. They assured me we'd have the recordings first thing on Monday morning."

Chapter Five

On Monday morning, Rhonda was surprised to find Martin already at his desk listening to the digital recordings of the interviews she'd done over the weekend.

"What time did you get in?" she asked once she got his attention.

Martin looked up, grinning like a kid who got one over on his teacher. "My wife had to catch an early bus to O'Hare for a business trip, so I came in after I dropped her off at six. I can't believe the crap these people were telling you. I thought the ones I interviewed were bad, but they were mild in comparison to this. Thank God you got the chick with the sex change. I don't know if I could have kept a straight face."

Rhonda laughed at Martin's description. Up until now, he'd seemed almost too straight-laced to be her partner. "These are mild compared to some of the other cases I've worked," she smiled at the memory of the high-profile cases she'd covered since she first investigated a murder.

Putting aside her mental ramblings, she continued. "There were a couple of the people this weekend, including Ms. Sex Change, who were happy about not having to deal with the late Mr. Potter. Unfortunately, they didn't strike me as the type to commit murder as a means to an end."

Martin got to his feet and stretched. "I've been told you go to the visitations as well as the funerals for the victims of the murders you investigate. I checked the obituaries this morning and saw the visitation for Mr. Potter is tonight. Does that mean we'll be going?"

"It's something I've found useful. It's interesting to sit back and listen to the conversations going on around us. You learn what everyone thinks when they have no idea anyone is listening."

This time it was Martin who laughed. "I was told…"

Rhonda shook her head in dismay. "Around here you believe only about half of what you hear about me. If you talk to Sheriff Cantwell, he'll tell you I'm unorthodox, but it gets the job done, so whatever I'm doing must be right. Changing the subject, did you get to interview everyone on your list this past weekend?"

"Yes, but I didn't get much information. This victim is really hard to read. How about you?"

Rhonda understood perfectly what Martin meant. Pete Potter seemed to be one of the most multi-faceted people she'd ever encountered. "I have three classmates left to talk to. Of course, they're all from the area. I would have gotten to everyone if I hadn't had to interview Pete's son, daughter and ex-wife. Talk about an odd family dynamic. Those three could all do one of those explosive talk shows that are on TV."

Before Martin could comment, Rhonda's phone rang. "Pohs here," she answered.

"This is Marcy Olson," the caller said, identifying herself.

She wouldn't have had to say anything. Rhonda would have recognized Marcy's throaty voice anywhere. As a leading defense attorney in town, Rhonda had been cross examined by her several times in the past.

"I wanted to make an appointment for my husband as well as myself to talk to you."

Rhonda nodded as though the caller sat across from her. "You certainly must understand I can't see the two of you together."

Marcy's silence led Rhonda to believe the woman hoped to put one over on her. "You interviewed Kathy and her daughter together, to say nothing of Donna and Chad. I don't see why David and I can't do the same thing. I doubt either of us will have a different story."

"You're not cross-examining me, Ms. Olson. Kathy was at the reunion when the murder was committed, but her daughter wasn't. It was the same with Donna and her son, Chad; they weren't at the reunion either. Considering you and David were both at the reunion you are both considered suspects. Unfortunately, I won't be able to see the two of you until either early tomorrow morning or after the funeral."

"David and I are both planning to go to the funeral, but I could come in before I go into the office tomorrow. Is seven thirty too early for you?"

Rhonda recognized Marcy's defensive move. "I can see no problem with that. I'm sure you need to be at your office by nine. If you and your husband would like to come in at the same time, I can take your statement first, getting you to work on time, then meet with your husband between eight and eight fifteen."

Again, the dead silence on the other end of the line told Rhonda she'd managed to outmaneuver the hip defense attorney.

"I guess that would work. I see no problem in bringing two vehicles to your office. We would have been driving to the funeral separately anyway. I'll be at your office at seven thirty. Knowing how you operate, I'm sure we'll see you at the visitation tonight."

Rhonda smiled confidently as she ended the call. Marcy Olson's interview would be the hardest one she'd conducted in this investigation so far. With the woman's skills, she'd guard her words closely.

"Do you want me to question Mr. Olson?" Martin asked when Rhonda turned to face him.

"I don't think so. Something tells me Marcy doesn't want me to talk to David alone. I've faced her in the courtroom before. She's a smart cookie, but I'm not so sure about her husband. From what I've heard, she married beneath herself."

"I know what you mean. I heard plenty out at that reunion site, especially when no one thought I was listening. From what I gathered; I'd like a chance to interview Tony Carpenter before you talk to the Olsons. I wonder if we could get him in here this afternoon."

Rhonda checked her notes and silently praised Martin for his intuition in this case. "That's a good idea. I think we should talk to him together. Can you get it set up while I go over the rest of your notes and recordings from the weekend?"

The smile crossing Martin's lips was proof Rhonda had made the right decision in giving her new partner so much trust. He was showing all the signs of becoming a top detective.

While Martin set up the appointment, Rhonda listened to the digital recordings, looking over the handwritten notes at the same time. From what she learned; it was no wonder Martin wanted to be in on the interview with Tony Carpenter.

Many of the classmates Martin talked with over the weekend alluded to the fact that, of all people, Tony was the one person who knew the most about his fellow attendees. Almost everyone who mentioned his name also said things like still waters run deep.

Before she finished listening to the weekend's interviews, Martin returned to her cubicle. "Were you able to set up an appointment?" she asked, turning off the audio disk.

"He'll be here in an hour. I hope that gives us enough time."

"More than enough," Rhonda agreed.

Rhonda's phone rang again. This time it was the medical examiner on the line. "Do you have the results of the autopsy?" she asked, knowing the body had been released to the funeral home earlier in the morning.

To her that meant the autopsy had been done over the weekend to put less stress on the family.

"I've got the tox report, otherwise I didn't need much. Your Vic was drunk at the time of his death. The blow to the head could have been the cause of death, but the coup de gras was the pair of women's thong underwear in his mouth. He would have died from the blow, but in the end he suffocated. I'm sure he went into the water postmortem."

"The panties put a new twist on this whole thing. Thanks for the information."

"Panties?" Martin questioned.

Rhonda related everything the medical examiner told her. "I haven't gotten through all of your interviews yet, but I don't know if I need to. Did you come up with anyone who knew about Pete's extra-curricular activities?"

Martin shook his head. "I had no idea about it until I listened to your interviews this morning. I think it was a very closely guarded secret."

~ * ~

Tony Carpenter arrived early for his appointment. As soon as he did, Martin ushered him into the interrogation room while Rhonda made certain the digital recording equipment was ready to capture Tony's every word.

Sitting at the table, she assessed the man they would be questioning. As a former wrestling star, he was larger than most of his classmates. Although not much over five foot nine he carried over two hundred and fifty pounds, definitely a very large man.

"How well did you know Mr. Potter?" Martin asked, beginning the questioning.

Rhonda was more than happy to sit back and let Martin be in the lead on this investigation. It gave her a chance to see her new partner in action and assess the man sitting across the table from them.

"I've stayed close enough to watch all my former classmates. Of course, that means I'm far enough away not to be involved. I'll admit Pete wasn't one of my favorite people. Let's face it, Pete was a bastard, not just because of the way he acted with every woman in the area, but also his business dealings."

"What do you mean by that?"

Tony smiled as if he harbored a secret he was reluctant to disclose. "I know you look at me as a fat man with little worth, but I keep a pretty low profile. I went to college in Montana on a wrestling scholarship. I'm the first to admit I wasn't the smartest kid in high school, but I worked my ass off to maintain a B average in college. My efforts didn't go unrewarded. I worked as an insurance agent in Wyoming for about ten years before I got transferred to the Minneapolis office. I worked my way up in the company and finally got tapped to work the office of the Wisconsin Insurance Commissioner in Madison."

"Undercover?" Rhonda asked, interrupting Tony's statement. "According to the bio we got from the reunion committee, you work in the shipping department of Rayovac in Madison."

A self-satisfied smile crossed Tony's lips. "I'm assuming this information goes no further than this room. Pete's been under investigation for almost a year now. We were planning to charge him with insurance fraud. In our investigation, we uncovered every unsavory aspect of Pete's life, including his trips to the cross-dressing bars in Madison. Oh yes, I know exactly what Geri told you about that. I should, she bragged about it to me Saturday night. She said I was still a fat slob and Pete always did get more action than me. It didn't matter what part he was playing. Of course, I already knew about it as well as how deeply he was involved in the transvestite world in Madison."

"This is one area where I'm completely in the dark." Martin

confessed. "Call me a hick from the sticks but what does the transvestite community have to do with this?"

"Pete was into some pretty dark stuff. He didn't just go to Madison with Geri. He went there alone to make some movies. I got into this world in my investigation. The money he was using to make them came from his fraud of the companies he represented in his agency."

Chapter Six

Rhonda sat at the funeral visitation, her mind filled with conflicting thoughts. Iris and Chad stood by the casket as the only surviving members of Pete's immediate family. Off to one side, Kathy and Donna sat with Pete's brother, Stanley, and sister, Angie. Not one person in the group appeared to be grieving over their loss.

Among the mourners were several classmates, at least the ones who stayed in the area. Added to the mix were several characters; the looks of which Rhoda never expected to see.

The one who stood out the most was a young man with long bleached blonde hair, pink stretch pants, striped slippers and a flat knit sweater. Beneath the sweater, he wore a bra he kept adjusting as though to keep it in place. While standing in line, he chatted with the people around him.

"I don't know what I'm going to do now that he's gone," the man lamented. "He was going to make me a star in his movie."

"A star, Les? How can you be a star? You've never done anything like this before," the person beside him questioned. "Besides, it wasn't really a movie, it was a documentary, and you weren't going to be acting, just being yourself."

"I was too going to be a movie star. He told me so. He said I was going to be his star. He knew talent when he saw it. The money I was going to make from this movie was what I planned to use to make my transformation complete. I hate being trapped in this body. I think Priscilla felt the same way I do."

Rhonda jotted a quick note to check out the name Pete used when he was pretending to be a woman. She had no doubt Tony would confirm Pete used the name of Priscilla with great regularity.

"With this movie not being made, I'm screwed. I'm going to have to stay in this fucking body for the rest of my life. I might as well kill myself. I can't stand being a man when what I really want is to be a woman."

The line moved on, making further eavesdropping out of the question. She nodded to Martin and knew he went out to check the memorial book to see if he could figure out who Les might be from the sign in.

Once up by the casket, Les made a scene Rhonda would not soon forget. He dropped to his knees, resting his head on the side of the gunmetal gray coffin and cried as though he'd lost either his best friend or his lover.

In comparison, the family stood dry eyed and composed.

Rhonda watched Les and saw the disgust in his expression.

Using her phone, Rhonda photographed the unique young man. By listening to the conversations going on around her she heard several names being associated with the mysterious Les. The one name she got was Patty Wallace. It was one she planned to check out tomorrow before the funeral. Perhaps Patty was the female name he used or maybe it belonged to another of the people Pete knew from Madison.

Rhonda's notes were finished when she looked, for the first time, at the funeral card supplied by the funeral home. Listed as the pallbearers were Mike Krumpy and Tom Coats, his classmates, John Potter and Alex Anthony she knew were nephews, but the names of Patty Wallace and Michelle Anders stuck out from the rest. It was evident they were some of his transvestite friends from Madison.

With the visitation over, Rhonda took a moment to talk with Iris and Chad. "I realize this is a hard time for the two of you," she began. "There are just a few questions I need to have answered. How did you decide on the pallbearers?"

"You'd have to ask Geri Salazar about that," Iris replied. "She approached us on Saturday night and said she had a list of things Pete wanted done. She gave us a complete file. I thought it was strange since he wasn't sick or anything."

"Do you still have the list?" Rhonda questioned.

Iris looked at her half-brother. "I didn't even open it," Chad confessed. "I certainly didn't want anything to do with it. It's bad enough we had to be here tonight and tomorrow. I brought it to the funeral home and told them these were supposedly my father's final wishes. I'm sure they must have them in the office."

Rhonda thanked Pete's kids and went to the office of the funeral director. "Chad tells me you have a list of Pete's final wishes," she said, once she seated herself across the desk from the director. "Can we see them?"

"I don't see why not. Of course, they wouldn't have had to give them to me, since Pete brought in the exact duplicate six months ago. He even went so far as to pick out the casket, the vault and the casket spray. I thought it very unusual for a forty-three-year-old man to make such arrangements. I told him I'd keep it on file, but I didn't think it would be relevant in thirty to forty years when the time came."

"What did Pete have to say about that?" Martin asked.

"He said he'd meet with me once a year and upgrade the list. The one thing he was adamant about was beneath his suit he wanted a pair of woman's thong underwear, a garter belt and a pair of silk hose. I've had some pretty weird requests before, but this one takes the cake. Just two weeks ago he brought in new underwear to replace what he gave me last year. He said it was more stylish."

The look on Martin's face mirrored Rhonda's shock at the situation.

~ * ~

Marcy arrived at the office at exactly seven thirty. Rhonda took a deep breath before entering the interrogation room.

"Thank you for coming in Ms. Olson. Do you have any idea who would have wanted Mr. Potter dead?"

"You'd be better off asking who'd want him alive. From what I could see he lived his life on his memories. If his old man hadn't given him that insurance agency, I don't know what he would have done for a living. I mean, in high school I did all of his homework. It was hard to dumb it down so he wouldn't come off as too smart. I hadn't thought about him in years, but right after the divorce, he showed up in my office and said he wanted to upgrade my insurance. When I told him to buzz off, he said I'd be sorry."

"Why would he say something like that?"

"He also said he'd be much better in bed than David. I told him if he tried anything like that I'd sue his ass off. That was the last time I saw him until Friday night. Even then he gave me a wide berth. I think I scared him shitless, and he couldn't cope. From what I heard, though, he hit on everyone else in a skirt, including our former class advisor."

Rhonda wondered if she should say anything about the strange mourners at last night's visitation. To her surprise, it was Marcy who brought it up.

"I've been hearing about Pete's trips to Madison for years. I guess I didn't want to believe it, but after seeing those weirdoes last night, I guess there isn't much doubt. I'm sure he's not gay, but he could have been a little AC/DC if you get my drift."

By the time the interview ended, Rhonda was questioning the need to talk to David Olson. It was evident Marcy put Pete in his place and he wasn't anxious to get close to the Olsons at the reunion.

Rhonda had about fifteen minutes to wait until David arrived at the office. To be truthful, Rhonda hadn't been able to place him from the weekend at the murder scene. As soon as she saw him, she realized she'd seen him several times and dismissed him as probably one of the farm workers.

David was listed as least likely to succeed, but it wasn't because he was a goof off. From what Rhonda could see, his intelligence was no match for that of his wife.

"You don't have to say it, Detective. I know you think I'm not an equal to my wife. I've tried to tell her that for years even though I love her with every fiber of my being."

"Did you know about Pete threatening Marcy?" Rhonda asked.

"I'm not the brightest bulb in the pack, I make no bones about it, but Marcy and I don't have any secrets from each other. Unfortunately, she is more forgiving than I am. I shouldn't let it bother me, but I do. I know she can do a lot better than being married to a part time janitor at McDonalds."

"With Marcy's success, do you really have to work?"

"Of course, I don't, but with the kids grown and in college, I had to have something to do. I've been a house husband for years. Don't get me wrong, I'm not ashamed of not supporting us. I enjoy doing the housework and I'm one hell of a cook. Of course, I've taken a lot of shit about it from the other guys in my class, but I doubt if any of them have the solid marriage Marcy and I enjoy."

"You said you aren't as forgiving as your wife. What did you mean by that?"

"I didn't mean I'd be out to kill the bastard. It's like Marcy's dad said once. She should have been the man in our relationship. I'm just too sensitive. I get my feelings hurt very easily."

Rhonda stayed in the interrogation room long after David left. In a way she felt sorry for the guy, but a nagging doubt ate at the back of her mind. Of everyone she'd interviewed, she had the strongest feelings about David.

~ * ~

The funeral wasn't one of the most largely attended ones she had ever been to. The first two rows of pews in the church were reserved for family. Iris sat next to Chad, but their mothers' occupied seats further back. Behind them were people Rhonda decided must be Pete's brother and sister and assorted nieces and nephews. Scattered throughout the rest of the front rows were a few classmates as well as an assortment of people Rhonda decided must be friends from his various trips to Madison. With them sat Geri Salazar, leaving no doubt about her knowing them well.

With everyone seated, the pallbearers entered the church and made their way to the front pew opposite the one where Iris and Chad were seated. The nephews were easy to spot. Both were well-dressed young men who looked comfortable in their clothes. Tom and Mike both looked as though the last thing they wanted to be wearing were suits and ties. On the sleeve of Tom's coat, she noticed a sewed-on tag he'd neglected to remove. She decided it was probably the first suit he'd bought in years. On the other hand, Mike's suit pulled across his shoulders, telling her it was something he'd bought years earlier and probably outgrown.

The last of the pallbearers were two women who looked more manly than womanish. They also wore suits, but rather than pants, they wore short miniskirts, four-inch heels, black stockings and white ruffled silk blouses.

They looked completely comfortable in these clothes, making Rhonda wonder if Pete looked as comfortable when he made his trips to Madison.

Further back, on the side of the church with the pallbearers, sat the man with the long blonde hair. Today his slippers had been replaced with black flats and the tweed skirt he wore was fashionable. Even so, she could see the unnecessary bra beneath the short-sleeved sweater he wore. It was evident the outfit was more fitting for winter than the sweltering heat of August.

After the sermon, Chad got to his feet and took a handheld microphone from the pastor. "My father was a difficult man to get to know. I'm just learning more about him. I've been told there are several of his friends who would like to say a few words today, so I turn the floor over to them." He handed the microphone back to the pastor and again took his seat.

The first to speak was Patty Wallace. "I know you all look at Pete's Madison friends with disgust. We're different from you, but it doesn't make us bad people. I'm a cross dresser and I'm not ashamed of it. My real name is Patrick and I have a wife and a family who are very understanding about this side of my life. Pete was like me, but he was afraid to let his friends know about this part of his life. He was trying to help us out, just as we were helping him understand his life. He was even planning to film a documentary about us to show the world we aren't freaks, we have real lives then we have our pretend lives. He was a good friend and I'll miss him terribly."

After what she'd heard the night before, it didn't surprise Rhonda when the bleached blonde got to his feet. "My name is Leslie Rapp. I'm different from the rest of the people Priscilla, I mean Pete, knew in Madison. I'm not a cross dresser. I'm in the process of becoming a woman. He understood and told me I'd be featured in his documentary. I was hoping it would make me enough money to be able to have the operation to complete the process. He understood me, like no one else has ever understood me in my entire life. He didn't judge me for the way I felt. I'm sorry he's dead. I wish he'd been my father. I look at his son and he looks like he's ashamed to be here. I'm not ashamed. I'm honored to have known such a wonderful man."

Leslie burst into tears and had to have help taking his seat.

Other members of the community of cross dressers from Madison also got up and talked about their feelings for Pete. It certainly put the man in a whole new light. So far, she saw him as a womanizer, a cross dresser, a mentor and someone who was cheating the very companies he worked for. She wondered what more she would uncover in this investigation.

With the funeral ended, Rhonda and Martin joined the line of cars making their way to the cemetery for the graveside service.

"What did you make of the people at the funeral?" Martin asked.

"I think the sentiments of Pete's Madison friends were very heartfelt. It's as though he was much more accepted in that world than he was in his hometown. It's highly possible his murderer is among the people we met today."

"I tend to agree with you. I think we need to talk to Tony again and see what else his investigation turned up. I'd like to know more about what constitutes insurance fraud and how they discovered it."

Rhonda nodded as they pulled into the cemetery. They were preceded into the narrow street leading to the gravesite by the hearse, the limo for the family, and eight individual cars. After parking, the funeral director opened the door for her. As she walked toward the canopy over the grave, she watched as the remainder of the mourners gathered.

Other than the blond, Leslie, from Madison, there were no tears, no hysterics. It seemed as though everyone there was reserved with quiet acceptance.

With the graveside services completed, Chad and Iris made a point of requesting Martin and Rhonda return to the church for the luncheon.

"Do you think we should be going back to the church?" Martin asked as they followed the rest of the cars out of the cemetery.

"Yes, I do. I usually attend to these things. You never know what someone will do or say in a more relaxed atmosphere."

Chapter Seven

If Rhonda thought she would get any information from the people at the funeral luncheon, she was mistaken. On the way back to the office, she and Martin discussed what little they actually learned during the day.

"What do you think of Pete's Madison friends?" Martin finally asked.

"Like we said earlier, I think they were the sincerest people there. Those men loved him. I'm sure it's like most of the people we all know. They have a hidden side and anyone not in that inner circle has no idea of their secret life."

"It was secret all right. I thought Chad and Iris were going to lose it when they saw the pallbearers come in. Those two guys in skirts were disconcerting for me. I can only imagine what they did to those two kids."

Rhonda agreed, but she also realized the society of people Pete mingled with in Madison had been of no danger to him. There, he wasn't living a life into which he didn't fit. There, he was himself and these people loved him for it.

"I think we need to look in a different direction," she finally said.

"I know what you're saying," Martin agreed. "I think we need to talk to Tony again. I'd like to know who Pete defrauded with his insurance business. I'm not even sure if I know exactly what insurance fraud is in the first place."

Rhonda nodded. With the visitation and funeral, she'd had little time to digest what Tony told them the day before. How could anyone defraud either their customers or the companies they worked for? To her it was incomprehensible.

"There's someone waiting for you," one of their fellow detectives advised them when they arrived back at the office.

"Waiting for us?" Martin questioned.

The detective nodded. "I saw this big man come in with a thick file. He asked if he could wait for the two of you to get back from the funeral. He said his name is Tony Carpenter and you might be interested in the information he brought in for you. I sent him to Rhonda's cubicle."

Rhonda smiled. Tony coming in could only mean he was willing to share the information in the file he'd compiled on Pete for the Insurance Commission. "Thanks," she replied. "We'll go back and meet with him right away."

Tony waited for them at Rhonda's cubicle. Despite the air conditioning, he was sweating profusely. As soon as they entered, Tony got to his feet.

"I didn't mean to just barge in, but I thought you'd be interested in the information I have on Pete. I called my superior in Madison and under the circumstances he gave me permission to turn it over to you. You have to know I didn't like Pete, but I do want to see his murder solved."

Rhonda glanced from Tony's beefy face to the thick folder on her desk. "That's a lot of information. How long has this investigation been going on?"

Tony took a handkerchief from his pocket and mopped his brow. "It was started about three years ago. Each incident was explained away by computer glitches, problems with the U.S. postal service, the list goes on and on. The biggest red flag came from a man who thought he'd bought a whole life insurance policy for his wife but found out it was term. When she passed away, the money he thought he'd have to use for her funeral wasn't there. The sad part was he'd been paying the premiums directly to Pete for over twenty years and to his father for at least twenty years before that. Pete learned how to do this from the master. His father had been doing it for years."

"Was he just skimming from life insurance policies?" Rhonda asked.

"Hell no. His main source came from car insurance premiums he never turned in to the companies. They didn't come to light until the state passed the law that to have your car licensed you had to have insurance. A lot of people just started calling the commissioner with complaints in the past six months when they were told their registrations had been revoked because they didn't have insurance coverage. Pete had been telling everyone he'd sent in the payments, and it must have been a glitch in the company's computer. When the insurance companies started lodging complaints, the commissioner decided it was time to shut him down. Unfortunately, someone shut him down for good before we could get to him."

"How long can we keep this file?" Rhonda asked.

"You can add it to your information permanently. I made you a copy of the complete file."

"I do thank you for this," Rhonda replied. "I hope we didn't keep you waiting too long."

Tony laughed. "In the summer, ten minutes is too long. I'm used to it. Even with the air conditioning, I tend to sweat. It's just something I've learned to live with over the years. My doctor tells me I wouldn't have such a problem if I lost about a hundred and fifty more pounds. I've already lost fifty, but it's a long hard journey." Rhonda completely understood what he was saying. She'd known several people who tried everything to lose weight and still hadn't achieved their goal.

"I put my business card in with the information. If there's anything you need me to clarify, you can call me on my cell phone."

After Tony left, Rhonda and Martin began going through the numerous complaints against Pete Potter and the way he conducted his business.

"I'm more confused than ever," Martin confessed. "We eliminate one set of suspects and now this opens a whole new list. There are complaints from almost every large company in the county, to say nothing of several individuals. To make matters worse, a lot of them go back to Pete's old man, just like Tony told us."

"There's so much information here, we should divide it up. It's almost time to quit for the day and I think we should start on this fresh tomorrow."

~ * ~

Rhonda was surprised to see Phil's truck parked in front of the house. Rather than go in through the front, she went around to the back where she was sure she'd find Phil and Mark sitting on the deck.

As soon as she stepped onto the deck, she saw Phil sitting in one of the deck chairs and Mark working on getting the charcoal going on the grill. Phil smiled at her and raised his beer in a mock salute. "You're late," he quipped. "I've already had my first beer."

"Don't tell me you're driving home," she said, knowing Phil would never be that foolish.

"Good grief no," Judy replied, coming out of the patio doors off the kitchen with a soda in her hand. "I told Pete if he was coming over here to bug you, I was coming along to be the designated driver. I know how Phil and Mark are when they get together." She winked slyly in the direction of the two men.

Rhonda laughed at her statement. "Let me go in and get comfortable and I'll join you guys. What are you planning to feed us, Mark?"

"Phil and Judy brought over the steaks and potato salad, so how could I say no to preparing the rest of the meal. We were just waiting for you to get here before we put the meat on the grill."

"Well, hold up on that long enough for me to at least get something to drink and wind down a bit." She turned to Phil. "I take it this was planned long before I got home. What's up?"

"We'll talk about it later," Phil assured her.

Rhonda didn't miss the look in her former partner's eyes. She knew exactly why he came tonight, and she knew she couldn't give him any information.

After changing into shorts and a tank with sandals, she poured herself a glass of iced tea before going back out to the deck.

"Now, I'll ask again, do I have to ask why you wanted to come over?" she inquired.

"I don't suppose you do," Phil commented. "I was wondering how the case was going."

Rhonda smiled at the man she knew so well. It was impossible for him to stay unconnected to this investigation. "You know I can't tell you anything. You're a suspect, or have you forgotten you were at the scene of the murder?"

"That's a whole new role for me and you know it. I miss not being in on everything."

Rhonda understood what he was saying. She missed his input on cases like this one but knew she couldn't ask for his guidance. Like she said earlier, he was a suspect.

"I thought I'd see you at the funeral."

"Never did like going to those things. You're the one who started that shit and I had to go along with you. Besides, Pete wasn't my good buddy, either in high school or lately. I'd look more like a curiosity seeker than anything else. From what I've heard, I missed quite a show. I also learned there weren't many classmates there."

Rhonda thought about the funeral with the two unusual pallbearers. In a normal case, Phil would have been amused by the group of Pete's Madison friends who came to pay their last respects.

"Let's change the subject," Mark suggested. "Even I can tell you're dying of curiosity on this one and Rhonda's nervous as a cat talking about it. When do you start your new job?"

Rhonda relaxed as she listened to Phil talking about how he'd be starting as liaison officer at one of the schools in Madison after Labor Day.

"Well," Judy began, "I for one will be happy when he finally goes back to work. Back when we were married, I signed up for better or worse, but not for twenty-four/seven. I know I complained when he was working all those long hours but having him under foot is worse yet. I'm hoping this vacation we leave on next week will take some of the tension away. I don't plan to do any cooking or so much as make a bed for a solid three weeks."

Mark put the steaks on the grill, then turned back to the conversation. "So where are you going on this fantastic trip?"

"We're driving out to California to see Judy's sister and her husband. Along the way, we're going to do all the touristy things. You know, Mt. Rushmore, Little Big Horn, Yellowstone, Yosemite, all the California stuff, the Grand Canyon and of course Las Vegas."

Judy laughed. "The Las Vegas thing is Phil's reward for putting up with my sister, Janet, for an entire week. He doesn't mesh well with her husband, Jeremy. To be truthful, I don't look forward to spending time with him either, but Janet and I are planning a lot of girl things to get us out of

59

the house."

Rhonda envied them for having the time to take a three-week driving tour out to the west coast and back. To have that much time to get away from it all would be heavenly.

The ringing of Rhonda's cell phone jolted her from the inner thoughts of travel. "Pohs here," she said, getting to her feet and going into the house for privacy.

"Detective Pohs, this is dispatch. We've had a call from a Mr. Chad Potter. He's calling from the home of his father, Pete Potter. The house has been vandalized. I realize it's a job for the city force, but the chief said to give you a call since you're investigating Mr. Potter's murder."

"Damn, I'll be right there."

She took a moment to change to jeans and a shirt before going back out onto the deck.

"Oh dear, I know that look," Judy said as soon as Rhonda came back to join the group. "You're not going to be eating with us. I've been married to a cop too long not to know you've been called out."

Rhonda could tell by the look in Phil's eyes, he envied the fact she was being called to investigate either a new crime scene or a new lead in the current case. For all any of them knew, tonight could be the lead that would either crack this case or instigate something Rhonda didn't want to have to deal with.

"I wish I could stay, but duty calls. You have a great vacation. I'll see you when you get back."

Phil got to his feet and kissed Rhonda on the cheek. "Give 'em hell, partner. You know I wish I could go with you. From the look on your face, I have a feeling this has something to do with Pete's murder. Of course, even if I were still your partner, I'd have to step aside."

Rhonda sighed deeply. If only Phil knew just how much she wanted him with her. Whatever this vandalism thing was, she had a feeling it was going to lead to so much more than she wanted to handle.

~ * ~

Being summer, daylight lasted far into the evening. With all the excitement surrounding the visitation and funeral, she hadn't even driven past Pete's former home.

Checking the address from dispatch, she was surprised to realize the house was in the middle of the historic district. Driving down the street where the showcase home was the local museum, Rhonda smiled at the number of homes either fully restored or in the process of undergoing a complete transformation.

In direct contrast was Pete's home. Paint peeled from the wood siding, the driveway wasn't paved and just beyond the sidewalk was a deep washout.

Chad and Iris stood on the wide front porch talking with two city officers. Rhonda no more than parked on the street opposite the house when Martin pulled in from the opposite direction.

She joined him as he headed up the sidewalk toward the broad front porch of the old home. The front picture window was completely shattered. To Rhonda's surprise, no one seemed to have made a move to enter the house.

"I'm Detective Pohs," she said, introducing herself to the two uniformed officers.

"I'm Officer Ransom and this is my partner Officer James, Ma'am. We were told we should wait for you to arrive before we did any investigation."

Rhonda nodded and quickly introduced Martin to the city officers. Once the formalities were taken care of, she turned her attention to Pete's kids, Chad and Iris. "What are the two of you doing here?" she asked, remembering them both saying they had no desire to take any of their father's belongings.

"We spent most of the afternoon with Dad's lawyer going over his will," Chad said. "After dinner we decided to come over here and see the place. We both know we can't completely wash our hands of Dad's things. I told Iris maybe there might be something she'd like to have. Besides, we have to know what we're dealing with before the auctioneer comes in to dispose of everything. When we got here, we found this." He pointed toward the smashed window.

"Did either of you go into the house?"

"Good grief no," Iris replied. "Chad had a key, but I didn't want to go in there. Who knows if someone might be in the house?"

"You were wise to call the police rather than walking in on something neither of you were prepared to handle."

"I have the key, Detective Pohs," Officer James said, as she approached the door.

Rhonda nodded. Just looking at the junk filled porch, she wondered how anyone could have ever crawled over all of it to be able to throw anything through the window.

A feeling of dread filled Rhonda's stomach. The young female officer drew her gun and entered the house with her partner. Rhonda followed them, listening to them announce that each room was clear. It was a relief to know no one was lying in wait for them to make a wrong move and put their lives in danger.

When the officers returned to the living room, Rhonda reached for the switch next to the door leading to the front porch. The disarray of the house came as no surprise.

Considering the amount of junk on the porch, the clutter of the living area of the home reminded her of the reality show Mark enjoyed watching, 'Hoarders'.

Shattered glass covered a dirty sofa piled high with old newspapers. Amid the sharp shards lay a brick with a note tied to it.

"Oh my god," Chad gasped from behind Rhonda.

She turned to see the look on the young man's face. It was immediately evident the condition of the home came as a complete shock. "Just how long has it been since you've been to visit your father?"

Chad's response was almost a whisper. "At least six years. I just couldn't tolerate his lifestyle. I can't believe it's gotten this bad in here. When I lived at home, things were always neat and clean, even after Mom left us. This is just more than I can even begin to process."

Rhonda made notes and watched as Officer James put on latex gloves before she picked up the brick. After removing the note and reading it, she handed it to Rhonda.

Turning away from Chad and Iris, Rhonda looked at the note. Printed in large block letters on the folded paper were the words *YOU*

WERE THE FIRST – YOU WON'T BE THE LAST.

The words were chilling. Did they mean this was the beginning of a serial killer or was this just a ruse to throw them off in the investigation?

Martin took the note from Rhonda and read it before slipping it into the evidence bag provided by the city officers. He started to say something, but Rhonda flashed him a look that she hoped told him to keep his mouth shut in front of Pete's kids. With a nod of her head, he followed her back outside leaving the others in the living room.

"What do you make of this?" Martin asked as soon as they were back on the sidewalk.

"I'm not sure. There are so many different directions we can go with this case; it could be anyone. Of course, I think what happened here tonight we could eliminate the people from Madison. I doubt any of them actually knew where Pete lived. Somehow, I feel like we're back to the people from the reunion."

"Are you saying you are having doubts about your former partner?"

Rhonda took a deep breath. She certainly couldn't rule Phil out. He was one of the classmates in attendance the first night of the reunion. From everything she learned from the interrogations of the classmates, she still doubted any of them were guilty. If anything, it was possible they too were targets.

While she was still trying to sort things out, she received another phone call. "Pohs here," she automatically answered.

"Rhonda, this is Sheriff Cantwell. Is Martin still with you?"

"Yes, he's right here."

Her heart pounded wildly within her chest. For some reason she knew exactly what her superior was about to say.

"We've got another murder. I need you to get over to the Hayes farm."

"Another murder on the same farm?" she asked, too stunned to say anything else.

"I'm afraid so."

Rhonda followed Martin back to his home on the east side of town. When he went into the house to tell his wife not to expect him back anytime soon, Rhonda placed a call to Mark to relay the same information.

"Are Phil and Judy still there?" she asked after giving Mark the needed details.

"Yes, they are. Do you want to talk to Phil?"

Rhonda thought for a moment wondering about the prudence of drawing her former partner into this. At the same time, she knew this was becoming a complicated case and she'd welcome his insight.

"What's going on?" Phil asked as soon as he took the phone from Mark.

"We've got another murder out at Jackson Hayes' farm."

Her statement met with dead silence on the other end of the line. "Who?"

"I don't know, but I'm sure it's not a coincidence. I'm just waiting for Martin to talk to his wife then we're heading out there. I certainly wish you were the one going with me tonight. I don't have a good feeling about this one."

"You'll do fine. Do you want us to postpone our vacation?"

Rhonda forced a laugh at the suggestion. "Of course, not. You deserve this. You have your cell phone, so I can keep you informed about what's going on. I see Martin coming. I'll talk to you later."

As she waited for Martin to get into the car, she thought about the phone call. For a moment, she felt like an unsure kid. Had she only talked to Phil to bolster her confidence or was she unsure about doing this without the partner she worked with since joining the county sheriff's department?

Emergency vehicles lined the side road with red and blue lights flashing in the twilight of the ever-increasing darkness. Showing her badge and identification to the county deputy stationed at the end of the driveway, Rhonda was allowed to drive past the barricades to get up to the house.

"Where have you been?" Sheriff Cantwell groused as soon as Rhonda parked her car and got out.

"We were downtown in the historic district at Pete Potter's house. It was vandalized earlier tonight. At least we thought it was tonight. That's when Chad and Iris discovered the shattered picture window."

In the glow from one of the dusk-to-dawn lights surrounding several of the buildings, Rhonda recognized Jackson and his wife talking to one of the many deputies swarming over the property. His shoulders were slumped as though someone sucker punched him in the gut and his wife clung to him as though he was her lifeline.

"What do we have here?" Martin asked, bringing Rhonda's attention back to the present.

"Jackson and his wife came home from going out to supper when they noticed their son lying outside the recording studio. They just took the body away. He was stabbed several times, and his throat was slit."

Rhonda remembered the young man who had been so helpful on Friday, only four days earlier. Silently, she cursed Sheriff Cantwell for allowing the body to be taken away from the scene before she had a chance to get there.

Coming toward her, Rhonda recognized Bob Masters, one of the other detectives working for the county.

"Cantwell said he called you and Martin in on this one," Bob said. "When we first responded I recognized the name. Do you think this has anything to do with the murder you're investigating?"

Rhonda thought for a moment before answering. "An hour ago, I would have said no, but now I'm not so sure. We just left Pete Potter's house. Someone smashed the front window with a brick. There was a note saying Pete was the first victim and there were more to come."

"Other than the location of both murders, what do you think Pete and Brandon Hayes have in common?"

"Until we do some checking," Martin said before Rhonda could wrap her mind around the situation, "the only thing in common is the class reunion. It's entirely possible it was the father and not the son who was the intended victim."

Rhonda could hardly believe what her partner just said. A stabbing was an up close and personal way to kill someone. Even from a distance, Jackson's six-foot two-inch frame and muscular build couldn't be mistaken for Brandon. The kid was shorter than his father and at least sixty pounds lighter.

While Bob and Martin discussed the possibility of the two murders on the Hayes farm being connected, Rhonda walked over to the blood stain indicating the murder site. With the dwindling light she wondered what she was missing.

Rather than stumbling around in the dark, she went back to her car for a flashlight. Returning, she looked around the perimeter of the recording studio. Rhonda had no idea what she was looking for, but prayed she'd find something to link the two cases to one another.

Martin called her name, but before she answered, something caught her eye. After putting on a pair of latex gloves, she bent down and retrieved a piece of folded white paper from beneath a rather large rock.

"What did you find?" Bob called.

Rhonda opened the paper. "I think this is either a copycat or the link we're looking for."

"What are you talking about?" Bob questioned.

Martin filled him in on the note attached to the brick thrown through the plate glass window at Pete's home.

The words on the paper were in the same block style and read, *TWO DOWN – HOW MANY MORE TO GO?*

Suddenly, Rhonda felt the need to find some common ground between forty-three-year-old Pete and twenty-one-year-old Brandon, other than they were both dead.

"Why my son?"

Rhonda turned to see Jackson standing behind her. "I don't know what to tell you. Other than being your son, do you know of any other connection he might have had to Pete?"

Jackson shook his head. "None that I know of. Brandon got his insurance from an office in Madison, the same as me. I doubt he even knew who Pete was before last Friday night. I wish I'd never planned that damnable party. What a bust."

"Is there a reason you don't buy your insurance locally?" Rhonda asked.

Knowing of the investigation by the Insurance Commission, she wanted to know what the local people had to say about Pete and his business practices.

"Let's put it this way, with this operation, I need a big agency. Besides, I've heard too many stories about Pete and his old man to do business with him. Even if his murder has something to do with his business practices, why would anyone want to kill my son?"

"I don't know of the connection yet but considering the location of the two murders and some of the other evidence we've gathered, we have to investigate every possibility."

Jackson left Rhonda and went back to where his wife was standing, sobbing silently. There was no way Rhonda could imagine the grief of losing a child. Instead of dwelling on it, she turned her thoughts back to the two notes she'd seen tonight. Hopefully, Sheriff Cantwell as well as Bob and Martin would agree with her that the contents of the second note should be kept confidential. If there were someone with a hit list, hopefully one or both of the notes would contain prints to bring an end to the nightmare before any more victims might die.

Chapter Eight

The alarm jolted Rhonda from too little sleep to start the day. It had been well after midnight by the time she finished her report to Sheriff Cantwell and took Martin home.

Reluctantly, she got up and made her way to the bathroom for a much needed wake up shower.

"It was pretty late last night," Mark said when she returned to the bedroom to get dressed. "Can't you call in and be a little late this morning?"

"Don't tempt me. This case is too complicated for me to think about being late."

"I'll get your breakfast ready while you get dressed. Is bacon and eggs all right with you?"

"Why don't you go back to bed? I'll grab something at one of the drive-thru places. I honestly don't have time to sit down and eat. I'm anxious to get to the office to see if the lab could lift any prints off the evidence we brought in last night."

"I don't like you not taking time to eat, but I understand your need to get into the office. Did you ever eat last night?"

Rhonda thought about the tacos she and Martin picked up on their way back into town early this morning. They certainly couldn't compare to the steaks she knew Mark prepared on the grill for Phil and Judy. "We got something on the way back."

"I'm almost afraid to ask what you had. Maybe it's best if I don't know. With luck you'll be off early enough to have a decent meal tonight."

Rhonda kissed her husband and headed toward the garage to leave. Within two blocks of work, she pulled into the drive-thru of the Golden Arches. As she waited for her food, she thought how much better Mark's proposed breakfast sounded in comparison to the breakfast burrito she just ordered. At least she knew the coffee would be better than the stuff they laughingly called coffee at the office.

"I wondered if you'd make it this morning," Sheriff Cantwell greeted her when she entered the office.

"When have I ever missed a day of work?" Rhonda retorted, both exhaustion and sarcasm sounding in her voice.

"Never, but Martin's in the hospital. As a matter of fact, he's in surgery. His wife called in this morning and said he had an attack of what he thought was indigestion. By the time she got him convinced to go to the hospital, it was almost too late. At least his appendix didn't burst."

"Something tells me you aren't going to send me home."

"Hardly, Bob Masters' partner, Joe Schaeffer, was in an accident last night after he left the Hayes farm. You're partnering with Bob for the rest of the week.

Rhonda thought about speaking with both Bob and Joe last night. Life certainly had a way of screwing up things when accidents and even illness happened unexpectedly. "How badly was Joe injured?"

"He was t-boned by a drunk driver. He'll be in the hospital for at least a week. He has two broken legs and internal injuries. The whole damn department is going to hell in a hand basket. Bob should be in shortly so you'll be able to put together your notes on what went on last night at the farm and you can bring him up to speed on the Potter case."

Rhonda could feel defeat sinking into her heart. It was one thing to break in Martin as her partner when Phil left, and quite another to have to work with someone new coming in halfway through a case.

Once in her office, Rhonda took a sip of her still hot coffee and opened the limp looking burrito. After one bite, she chucked the remainder of the uneaten breakfast into the trash.

"Don't tell me that's your breakfast." Bob said from the doorway to her cubicle.

"I'm afraid so. At the time it sounded like a good idea, but one bite told me I'd been better off letting Mark make breakfast for me."

"You were right to dump that crap. Why don't you let me buy you a decent meal while you bring me up to speed on the Potter case?"

Rhonda's stomach growled, giving Bob his answer. She grabbed her notebook and followed him out to his car.

The small café Bob chose was relatively quiet. The breakfast crowd was long gone and the lunch bunch at least two hours away. In the front of the room, tables of friends were enjoying a morning of coffee and gossip, leaving the table at the back vacant.

"Are you still serving breakfast?" Bob asked when the server approached their table.

The girl winked. "We offer breakfast all day. Can I start you with coffee?"

Rhonda nodded and checked the menu. She and Mark had eaten here one Sunday after church and the peach cobbler pancakes made her mouth water in anticipation.

By the time the waitress returned with their coffee, Bob decided on stuffed French toast, and they had time to talk before their food arrived. "Now, what makes you think these two murders are connected?" Bob asked.

"You saw the note we found at the Hayes farm, and we told you about the one tied to the brick at Pete's place. It reminded me of a case that happened in Milton about twenty years ago."

She watched as the light of recognition flashed in Bob's eyes. "I'd forgotten about that one. I was just a kid, but didn't the brother murder his sister?"

"That's right. He left her dead in the basement and took off. As I recall, a county sheriff pulled him over on Highway 51 and saw the bloody knife and he said he'd been fishing."

"How did they catch him?"

"If my memory serves me right, he stopped at the rectory and gave himself up to the priest. When the city cops searched his room, they found he had a hit list of just about everyone in town."

"So, what does that case have to do with ours?"

Rhonda took a deep breath. "Between Martin and me, we interviewed all the classmates at the reunion and started looking into Pete's business practices. After getting that note at his place last night, I'm beginning to think we're looking in the wrong directions."

"You might be right. Are you sure where that guy is now?"

Rhonda realized she hadn't thought about the old murder in years. "He's an inmate at the state mental hospital. Every couple of years he makes an appeal to get out but, so far, there's no halfway house willing to take him."

"I guess that means we have to start from scratch. Do you have any ideas?"

Rhonda took a sip of her coffee as she contemplated her answer. "I think this murder, like that old one, has someone close to home behind it. For some reason I think we're dealing with someone with a grudge against the people at the reunion."

"That doesn't explain why anyone would kill the Hayes kid."

"There's got to be a link somewhere. We just have to find it before it's too late. We certainly don't want bodies piling up here. If we're dealing with a serial killer, this could be just the tip of the iceberg."

The waitress returned with their breakfast, giving Rhonda time to think about the answers she needed.

Before they could resume their conversation, Rhonda's phone rang. It came as a surprise to find Phil on the other end of the line.

"We got a late start," Phil began. "We just heard the news about the Hayes kid on the radio. What the hell is going on? Do we need to stay in town? Do you need my help?"

I'd kill for your help on this one, but I'm on my own. "There's no need to change your plans. As a matter of fact, it's just as well you're out of town right now. I'll fill you in on everything when you get back. Hopefully we should be able to put this one to bed before you and Judy get home."

By the time they ended the conversation, Rhonda was convinced it was best for Phil and Judy to be out of town. It was a shame the remainder of the classmates and their families couldn't be out of town as well. Of course, she knew it wasn't practical since whoever the fiend behind this was didn't have to act immediately.

"Do I have to ask who the caller was?" Bob asked, his smile genuine. "You and Phil were partners for quite a while. I'm willing to bet he wants in on this one."

"I wouldn't bet against you. He understands he can't help, but I know he feels guilty leaving this morning for a three-week vacation."

"You're leaving out the fact he was at the farm when Pete's murder happened. I'm sure it was hard for him to be questioned as though he was a suspect."

Rhonda nodded. She was the first to admit she missed Phil. Now having to once again change partners for this case was making her nervous.

~ * ~

"You look beat," Mark said as soon as Rhonda came home.

"I am. This case sucks big time. Not only do I miss Phil, but when I got in this morning I found out Martin is in the hospital. I spent the entire day bringing Bob Masters up to speed. To make matters worse, the lab is backed up so they couldn't get the evidence from last night processed."

Throughout dinner, Rhonda vented her frustrations without giving away too many of the details regarding her two current cases.

"How about a change of subject" Mark suggested as he set their steaks on the table.

"I hope it's good news, I can sure use some."

Mark's smile put Rhonda at ease. "I had a call from the school in Las Vegas. They want me to come out next week for an interview."

Rhonda's mind began to spin. "If you were to get it, when would you be expected to start?"

"They want to have someone in place for the second semester for the basketball and baseball seasons."

They'd talked about it before, and Rhonda knew this was something her husband wanted. If he got the job, she'd have to ask Sheriff Cantwell to put in a good word for her with one of the law enforcement agencies out there. She knew if this chance for advancement came through and she didn't have these two cases solved, she'd be the one who would have to stay behind to tie up all the loose ends.

Chapter Nine

The next morning, when Rhonda arrived at the office, the file regarding the twenty-year-old murder case they'd discussed yesterday was on her desk.

"I looked up that case we were talking about yesterday," Bob said from behind her.

"I see that. Do I have to ask if you've read through all the information yet?"

"You could, but the answer would be no. I requested it from records last night before I went home. I just got in myself. I was hoping we could go over it together."

Rhonda nodded. She'd also decided to look into the old case for similarities with the mess she was now involved in. "I guess great minds do travel in the same circle. You just beat me to the punch."

Together they sat down with the file between them. The facts within its pages brought back the fear she felt as a teenager when it first happened.

"I'd forgotten most of this stuff," Bob commented. "It's hard to say what would have happened if he'd carried out the hits of the other people on his list before he killed his sister."

"I hadn't thought of that. Looking at this list, it was an extensive one. There's everyone here from classmates to the postmaster and the pharmacist. I have a feeling after he killed his sister, he realized what he'd done was wrong. Unfortunately, if my gut feeling is right, our killer is enjoying clearing his list."

Bob sat back, as though contemplating what Rhonda had just said. "So, what do you think the connection between Pete and the Hayes kid could be?"

"It's got to be someone with a grudge against both of our victims. The age difference has me baffled. What does a middle-aged skirt chasing, cross dressing crook have in common with a clean-cut kid like Brandon? I worked with him when we were doing the investigations into Pete's murder and wouldn't call him anything other than a straight arrow."

"Do you think his murder could be because of his work with the department? Is it possible whoever the killer is may have thought the kid might have listened to the interviews? If so, Brandon might have had an idea who the killer could be."

"I doubt it. As far as I'm concerned, rather than finding a murderer, we found out the truth about the real Pete Potter. The classmates were evenly split between loving him, hating him, and not giving a damn about him. There has to be something we haven't uncovered yet. I still think we need to make a trip to Madison and talk to the cross dressers Martin and I met at the funeral. For some reason, I think it's a good place to start looking for answers."

~ * ~

Even though the Hayes murder wasn't her case, Rhonda insisted on attending the visitation as well as the funeral with Bob.

"I think it's a good place to start looking for answers."

"I've heard about you and Phil doing this," Bob said, once they paid their respects to the family. "Do you really get any leads?"

"Not always, but you never know when you're going to hear something or get some information we can glean. In one case I investigated, one of the murderers actually came to the visitation. Another time, one of the floral arrangements was a big clue."

Bob broke into a wide grin. "Guess everyone in the department knew about that rocking chair and scarecrow. I saw the pictures. That was one of the most gruesome things I ever saw or heard of for that matter."

The line of mourners at the visitation included several of the young people from the area who'd gone to school with Brandon. Mingled in with the young adults, either engrossed in college classes or embarking on careers, were their parents, classmates of Brandon's parents and assorted family members.

Rhonda couldn't help but compare this visitation to the one she'd attended earlier in the week for Pete Potter. There, with the exception of the one young man from Madison, there were no tears. Here, teenagers as well as adults cried openly, and floral arrangements covered every available space.

She was headed toward the mortician's office when she met Dave and Marcy Olson. "I can't believe something like this could happen," Marcy lamented. "Brandon went to school with our kids, and I didn't think he had an enemy in the world."

"I tend to agree," Rhonda said. "This is going to be a very interesting investigation. How well did you know Brandon?"

"Just from school functions. He was in the same class as our son, Jason, from kindergarten through graduation. Of course, they lost touch when Jason went on to college at UW Madison."

"Is Jason here?" Rhonda inquired.

"He's going to come to the funeral tomorrow. He had something going tonight. You know how young people are, they tend to keep too busy."

The line moved on, and Rhonda went on with her original plans. She found Chuck Hadley, the owner of the funeral home, in his office. "Do you have a minute, Chuck?"

"Sure Rhonda. Please don't tell me there's another gruesome arrangement out there."

Rhonda managed a weak smile. "Hardly. I was wondering if you could get me a couple of addresses or phone numbers, whichever you have."

"What are you looking for?"

"I'd like the contact information for Pete Potter's two pallbearers from Madison. If my memory serves me right their names were Patty Wallace and Michelle Anders."

"I should have the information in my database, but with the size of this visitation, I'm afraid you'll have to wait until morning to talk with my secretary. She can access it for you. Tonight we're just too overwhelmed to go looking for something she can find with just a minimum of keystrokes."

"I understand. Here's my card. You can send me the information via e-mail. Since Bob and I will be attending the funeral tomorrow, we wouldn't have time to work on it until tomorrow afternoon."

"Bob? What happened to Martin?"

"It's just my luck, not only was I working with a new partner at the beginning of this investigation, now I have a replacement, since Martin needed emergency surgery."

"That's too bad for you. From what I've heard you're up to your armpits in alligators on this one."

Rhonda thanked Chuck and returned to her seat next to Bob. "Hear anything interesting?" she asked.

"I don't know how interesting it is, but it did sound strange. I heard one of the girls say she wasn't surprised about the murder since Brandon was such a homophobe."

"Brandon? That's certainly hard to believe. He certainly didn't come off that way when we were doing the investigation. He seemed quite normal to me. I guess it's something we need to talk to Jackson and Cindy Hayes about after the funeral."

~ * ~

It was late when Rhonda finally returned home. She smiled to find Mark waiting for her. "How did you know I didn't eat supper?"

"Honey, I've been married to you too long not to know your habits. As late as it is, I thought we'd just have BLT's. Why don't you go in and get comfortable while I finish frying the bacon?"

Once she'd donned sweat shorts and a tee shirt, Rhonda returned to the kitchen.

"It's such a nice night, do you mind if we eat out on the deck?" Mark asked.

Rhonda smiled. "I think that would be lovely. Any chance we have some wine chilling?"

"It just so happens I do. I know how much you like Lambrusco, so I put a bottle in the refrigerator this morning. Hopefully it's going to make the news I have for you a little easier to take."

She swallowed hard, wondering what Mark was about to tell her.

On the deck, the table was set with two glasses of wine, triple decker BLTs on colorful paper plates, a bowl of chips with dip and a tray of fresh veggies. "You done good. I'm almost dreading what you're going to tell me."

"It's not bad," Mark quickly replied. "I got a call from Las Vegas today. Rather than a face-to-face interview, the head of the HR department did one over the phone. To make a long story short, I have the job, if I want it. They want me to fly out there tomorrow and meet with the rest of the staff. I know this is a bad time for me to be gone, especially with you in the middle of this god-awful case, but…"

Rhonda put her finger to Mark's lips. "We knew this was coming. To be truthful, it's good to know we don't have to wait for a decision from the school. What difference does it make if you go out tomorrow or next week? You've worked hard for this. I promise I won't waste away to nothingness if you're not cooking for me. I think it's great they want you to come out and get acquainted with the people you'll be working with."

"That's not all. They want me to start at the beginning of the basketball season, no later than the end of October."

"What about your job here?"

"I talked to the head of the athletic department. Since he knew I would be leaving at the beginning of second semester, he's been looking for a replacement for me. I resigned as of the first of October. That should give us time to put this house on the market and while I'm out in Las Vegas I can start looking for a place for us to live."

Rhonda's stomach began to do flip-flops. The way this case was going, she doubted she'd have anything solved before it was time for Mark to leave to begin his new position. At least she'd have a place to live, since with the economy the way it was she doubted if they'd have their house sold that quickly.

Chapter Ten

The funeral was no more enlightening than the visitation the night before. Although Rhonda wanted to question Jackson and Cindy regarding the overheard conversation about Brandon being a homophobe, she refrained. Today wasn't the time to follow up on that lead. The couple just buried their son. Her inquiries could wait until another day.

After the luncheon, she excused herself to take Mark to the bus station to catch the airport shuttle that would get him to Chicago in time for his five o'clock flight to Las Vegas.

As she watched the bus pull out onto the highway, she realized the merry-go-round she was on seemed to be speeding up at an overwhelming rate. On her way back to the office, she stopped at the real estate office and made an appointment to meet with the realtor when Mark returned home. From there she went to Sheriff Cantwell's office to talk to him about her resignation.

"Do you have anything new on the Potter/Hayes case?" the sheriff asked as soon as she entered his office.

"We're working on a couple of new leads, but nothing solid at this point. I'm not here to talk about that. Mark left for Las Vegas this morning. I know I told you he was hoping to start at the beginning of second semester if they hired him. He got a call yesterday and they hired him. The catch is it seems they want him to be out there for the start of basketball season."

"That's interesting. Are you telling me I'm going to have less than two months to replace you?"

"In a way. I'm not making any definite plans until this case is solved. If Mark has to go out to Las Vegas alone, then so be it. I refuse to leave this one in someone else's hands. It's a shame Martin got sick, but I think Bob and I can come up with a solution, I just don't know when."

"I can understand the way you feel. It's going to be hard replacing you, especially since we had to find someone to fill Phil's shoes at the beginning of the summer. Do you still want me to contact my friends in Las Vegas?"

"I'd appreciate it, but I know getting a place out there could take a while. Luckily, we have enough in savings to see us through if I don't get a position right away. I do want to thank you for understanding."

~ * ~

Once Rhonda returned to her office, she checked her email. The information she wanted on Patty Wallace and Michelle Anders was in her inbox. Unfortunately, there was no contact for Leslie Rapp. With a way to contact Patty and Michelle, Rhonda was sure she'd be able to get a lead on Leslie from one of them.

"Did you get your information?" Bob asked.

"Yes, I did. I was just getting ready to call Madison and see if we can set up an appointment for tomorrow."

"Well, while you were seeing your hubby off, I was listening to more of the interviews from the reunion. I certainly can't seem to come up with anyone who might be responsible for these murders."

"I know what you mean. At least with Mark out of town I'll have more time to devote to trying to solve this case."

"Just don't forget to devote some time to taking care of yourself."

Rhonda laughed at the comment. It seemed like all the men in her life were on the same track.

After checking the clock, Rhonda placed a call to Patty Wallace, while Bob did the same for Michelle Anders.

"This is Patty," a very masculine voice answered her request to speak with the woman.

"This is Detective Pohs from the Rock County Sheriff's office."

"Oh yes, we met at Pete's funeral. How can I help you?"

"We've had another murder, and we think the two of them are connected. My partner is contacting Michelle, and we were wondering if we could have a meeting with the two of you, possibly tomorrow. We'd also like to meet with Leslie Rapp, that is, if you know how to contact him."

"I'd have to talk to Michelle, but I can contact Leslie. When and where would you like to meet?"

"I was thinking about sometime tomorrow. I can leave the time and place up to you and the others. I'll give you my cell number and you can get back to me with the details."

With the call ended, Rhonda wondered if she'd ever hear from Patty again. Straightening the files on her desk, she got up to check in with Bob before going home for the night.

"Did you get a hold of Michelle?" she asked.

"I left a voice mail. How did you do?"

"I talked to Patty. He said he'd be calling me back after being in contact with Michelle and Les. I hope I'm reading this guy right. If so, we'll probably be making a trip to Madison tomorrow."

~ * ~

Rhonda didn't like the idea of walking into the empty house. It wasn't the first time Mark was out of town and she was alone, but this case had her beside herself with questions that had no answers.

She no more than began to raid the refrigerator than her cell phone rang. "Pohs here," she automatically answered while pulling out a bowl of macaroni salad.

"This is Patrick Anniston from Madison," the now familiar voice replied.

"Thank you so much for getting back to me." "I've talked to both Mike and Les," he started.

"Mike?"

"That's Michelle's real name. They've consented to meeting with you tomorrow at ten. Can you meet us at the Perkins on Fish Hatchery Road?"

"That shouldn't be a problem, but won't that conflict with your jobs?"

"Not at all. Mike runs his own Internet Company and I'm a freelance writer. Our schedules are fairly open. As for Les, that poor kid is so messed up he can't keep a job. He lives with his folks. Thank goodness they're able to help him."

"I'm writing all this down. I'll contact my partner and meet you for coffee. I doubt we'll have any problem recognizing you."

"Don't be so certain. When we go out it's certainly not as Patty and Michelle. It doesn't matter. We'll be able to recognize you from the funeral."

The masculine laughter on the other end of the line brought a smile to Ronda's lips. Had she really expected to see these two guys coming to the restaurant in full drag? Of course, she had. Now she remembered Patty's words at the funeral when he said his wife was very understanding of his sexual needs.

After filling a bowl with the salad and pouring herself a glass of wine, she went out to the deck and placed a call to Bob.

"I just got off the phone with Patrick Anniston," she informed him. "All three of them are able to meet with us tomorrow morning at ten."

"I was hoping that's what you were going to tell me. Before I left work, I cleared everything with Cantwell. Since the meeting is set for ten, I'll be picking you up at your place at nine. There won't be much we can accomplish at the office before we have to leave so you might as well take the time to sleep in."

"Thanks for talking to Cantwell for us. I was going to call him next. I'll see you in the morning."

With the call to Bob completed, Rhonda finished her wine as well as her dinner and went in and drew a hot bath. This was one night when soaking in a tub of hot water sounded like something she needed.

She'd just slipped into the sudsy water when the house phone rang. Since she expected Mark to call, she'd brought the portable handset into the bathroom with her.

"Hello sweetheart," she answered. "How was your flight?"

"Now wouldn't you have been embarrassed if there was someone other than me on the end of the line?" Mark teased.

"I took a chance. Besides, who else would be calling me this late?"

"Guess you're right. It was a good flight, and the school administrator met me at the airport. They've put me up in a nice hotel off the strip. Did you find the surprise I left for you in the refrigerator?"

"If you're talking about the macaroni salad, yes I did and it made a great supper. I even had a glass of wine to go with it."

"So, did I wake you?"

"No. I'm soaking in the tub. I wish you were with me and we could play with the bubbles."

"No more than I do. How's the case going?"

"Bob and I are going to Madison tomorrow to meet with the three guys who were friends with Pete. We're hoping they can shed some light on this situation."

"Are you telling me you're meeting with the he/she's?"

"Don't call them that. Patrick and Mike are transvestites and Les is little more than a sexually confused teenager. They knew Pete better than almost anyone else we've interviewed."

"Well, I wish you luck. Thank goodness this is your job and not mine."

"What do you mean by that?"

There was a pause on the other end of the line. "I'm just not comfortable with all this mixed-up sex stuff."

Rhonda laughed at Mark's comment. "If that's the case, and to be truthful, I rather doubt it, maybe you should rethink moving to Las Vegas. They have some strange goings on out there."

"I'm not a homophobe or anything like that, honey. It's just this is something I don't understand."

The word homophobe jogged Rhonda's memory of what was said at Brandon's funeral. "Why would you use the word homophobe?"

"I guess it's something I picked up from the kids at school. There's been a lot of talk about people who are gay and those who just can't accept it. The kids in the latter category are called homophobes by their friends. Why do you ask?"

"At the visitation, one of the girls called Branson Hayes a homophobe. I was going to speak with his parents about it but haven't called them yet."

"I don't know anything about the kid other than he played basketball for Clinton while he was in school. The only reason I know is that we played a non-conference game against them a few years back. He was the center and one of the most talented players I've seen in a long time. I heard he got a scholarship to Oshkosh to study media. I never heard if he was playing ball for them, though."

Rhonda changed the subject and filed away the information she'd received from Mark for future reference.

By the time they finished their conversation, the water in the tub went cold. After draining out the water, she quickly washed her hair under the shower and prepared to go to bed.

After making a check of all the doors and windows, she settled down for the night. It was well past midnight when the sound of breaking glass woke Rhonda.

She got out of bed and ran to the front room just in time to see a vehicle speeding down the road. At her feet was a brick with a note attached.

Chapter Eleven

Rather than touch anything and contaminate evidence, Rhonda called dispatch and Sheriff Cantwell. Almost as soon as she hung up, she could hear the sirens screaming down her street. For the first time she realized she hadn't taken the time to put on a robe to cover her night-shirt. Before the officers could get to her front door, she rushed back to the bedroom and grabbed her robe.

"What can you tell us about this, Mrs. Pohs?" the young officer asked as he entered the house.

It was hard to go from professional cop to victim and she weighed her answer carefully. "I was sleeping when I heard glass breaking. I saw a car speeding away, but I couldn't tell you much about it, other than it was an older vehicle."

"Have you touched anything?"

Rhonda rolled her eyes in exasperation. "Of course, I haven't."

"Are you alone in the house?"

"Yes, I am. My husband is out of town on business."

"Do you think this has anything to do with your husband's business?"

Rhonda let out a loud sigh. It was evident these cops had no idea who they were talking to. "Most definitely not. I'm the lead detective on the Potter/Hayes murder case. I'm sure whatever that note says it's meant for me."

"Just what the hell is going on here?" Sheriff Cantwell demanded as he rushed into the house.

Rhonda turned to confront her boss. "I think our murderer is beginning to either feel the heat or is teasing us. You know, sort of a catch me if you can scenario."

"Sheriff Cantwell, why are you here? This isn't something for the county to be investigating…"

"Did you just say that young man?" Sheriff Cantwell questioned. "Detective Pohs is involved in a high-profile murder case. Since the two murders she's investigating both happened within the county, anything that happens to her is of my concern."

Turning back to Rhonda, he continued. "Have you looked at the note wrapped around this rock?"

"Of course, I haven't. I was waiting for the forensics team to get here. I'm not a rookie, for goodness sake." She glanced toward the two city officers who questioned her earlier. "Besides, everything has happened so fast I didn't have time to even find a pair of gloves. I wouldn't want to contaminate anything."

More officers arrived along with the forensics team. After photos of the scene were taken, one of the officers unwrapped the note from around the rock. With the others in the room, Rhonda read the words printed in large block letters. – I WON'T MAKE THIS EASY FOR YOU – MY LIST IS GETTING SMALLER – ARE YOU ON IT DETECTIVE POHS?

"I don't think it's wise for you to stay here tonight," Sheriff Cantwell observed. "It's evident the killer knows where you live. You can consider yourself threatened."

"I can't leave the house like this. I'll be fine, I promise. I'll get the window boarded up and go back to bed. Since Bob and I aren't leaving for Madison until nine tomorrow morning, I'll have time to make arrangements to have the window replaced."

"You could do all that from a hotel."

"You make it sound like I'm a scared little mouse. I wasn't assaulted. I was merely warned. This guy is making a statement. Like I said, he's playing a game of catch me if you can. I won't fall into his trap. I promise, I'll be perfectly fine."

"You're damn right you will. I'm having a guard stay here with you tonight and there will be patrols in your neighborhood all night. Do you think you should call Mark and tell him what's going on?"

"There's no sense in getting him upset about something he can do nothing about. Right now he needs to concentrate on his meetings in Las Vegas."

~ * ~

By nine the next morning, Rhonda was more than ready to go to Madison with Bob. She'd arranged with the next-door neighbor to meet the window people. Even though she was running on little or no sleep, she was anxious for the meeting with the three men from Madison.

"I heard what went on here last night," Bob said once she slid into the passenger's seat of his car. "This guy is really getting brazen. I do agree with Sheriff Cantwell, until Mark gets home you shouldn't be alone. I talked with my wife, and she insisted when we get back from Madison you should pack a bag and come to our place."

"B–but I can't."

"You can and you will. It's an order, not only from me but also from Sheriff Cantwell. End of discussion."

Rhonda seethed over being manipulated by both her partner and her boss, but finally agreed staying by herself wouldn't be the smartest thing she'd ever done.

The parking lot at Perkins was almost empty. Bob parked close to the door and came around to her side of the car to play the part of a perfect gentleman.

Once inside the restaurant, a man dressed in jeans and a short-sleeved button-down shirt came up to her. "I'm Patrick Anniston, Detective Pohs."

Rhonda stared at the man for a minute, trying to equate him with Patty from the visitation and funeral. Slowly, the resemblance between the man and the woman he enjoyed portraying began to merge.

As she followed him to the table, she was greeted by a very masculine Mike, as well as Leslie, who looked nearly the same as he had on the previous occasions they'd met.

"What can we help you with?" Mike asked.

"We're trying to find someone with a connection to two different victims. Can any of you remember someone who might have been bothering Pete?"

"I know most of the people who come to the club, but during the last few weeks of school at the University we started getting a younger crowd in here. There were a couple of cross dressers, but there were also some guys who were openly gay. They just didn't mesh with our group. I think someone said something to one of them, and they didn't come back again."

"I know what you're thinking," Leslie blurted out. "You're thinking I don't belong there either, but these guys have taken me under their wings and they're very supportive."

"I don't want you to think I'm judging you," Rhonda said, reaching across the table to squeeze his hand. "More than anything, I'm concerned about you. I know Pete promised you a lot that isn't going to happen now."

"Don't worry about Les," Patrick said. "I had a call from Pete's son, Chad. He was concerned about Les too, and told him when the estate is settled there will be money available for Les to have the operation."

"You're kidding, right?" Bob questioned.

"We were shocked too, but the kid said he didn't want the money and neither did his sister. Once everything is settled, they're planning to give everything away and decided Les was a worthy cause."

"I think that's wonderful," Rhonda said, once she regained her composure. "What I want to know is if you have any idea about the identity of these college students?"

Mike shook his head. "We've been talking about this since last night after Pat got your call. These guys stuck out like sore thumbs, but we never got any names. Since they were asked to leave the club, we thought that was the end of things. There are a lot of gay bars where these guys can go to have a good time and hook up."

"Come to think of it," Pat said, "there was one kid who really got on Pete's case. Before they left, he was screaming at Pete and saying he was nothing more than a fuckin' freak who wasn't even man enough to admit he's gay."

"What did Pete say?" Rhonda asked.

"He tried to laugh it off, but I think the kid freaked him out. He left the bar right after it happened. In fact, he didn't come back for about three weeks. He was in contact with Les about the documentary, but only by phone. When he did come back to the club, he seemed jittery for the first couple of times."

"Was Geri there when this happened?"

"That was the strange thing. That night Pete came without her. Of course, there were other times he came alone, but this was on her regular night. He said she was sick and couldn't make it. I have to admit it seemed funny not to have her with us. She's a great chick to party with."

Rhonda wrote notes as quickly as she could and was glad Bob remembered to bring a digital recorder to catch every word of their conversation.

After finishing their lunch, Bob and Rhonda headed back to the office.

"What do you make of that?" Bob asked.

"I think I have to talk to Geri again. The way it sounded when I interviewed her, Pete didn't ever go to Madison without her. Later, when I talked to Tony Carpenter, he said Pete often went without her. I didn't give it much thought at the time, but maybe she didn't know him as well as she thought she did."

Chapter Twelve

"Are you sure you aren't hurt?" Mark asked when she called his cell after they got back to her house.

"I'm positive. Bob and I had to go to Madison to do an interview this morning and when we got back, the window was repaired. I just wanted to let you know I won't be here if you should call the house phone."

"Why not?"

"Between Bob and Sheriff Cantwell, they convinced me it wasn't safe for me to stay here alone. I'm going to go over to Bob's place. His wife actually insisted on it."

"I agree. Do you want me to cut things short out here?"

"Absolutely not. I have a meeting with the realtor set for Saturday morning. Thank goodness you're such a good housekeeper. I don't have much to do to get this place ready to go on the market. Since our neighbor was here to meet the window people, she cleaned up the broken glass, so we're good to go. Have you found anything for us to rent when we get out there?"

"Not yet. I've been meeting with the people from the school steady. I talked to the football coach and he's taking me out looking on Saturday. I should be back home Sunday afternoon on the bus that gets in at five. I'll see you then. If you need me for anything, just give me a call and I'll change my reservations."

"I doubt I'll need you. I have a feeling I won't be able to come home without someone with me until you get back. I can hardly wait to hear all about what went on in Vegas."

"He wants to come running back home, right?" Bob asked when Rhonda hung up the phone.

"How did you guess?"

"It's what I'd want to do if I were in his position. I can't imagine being so far away from home with all the drama happening back here."

"Mark knows I can take care of myself. Besides, he understands this is part of the job. With you and Cantwell looking out for me, what can happen?"

She gave Bob a glance she hoped would say she was confident, but inside she had her doubts about everything going on in her life.

Bob sat in the kitchen sipping a glass of iced tea while Rhonda finished packing to go to his place for the night. It only took one call to Bob's wife, Francine, to tell Rhonda it hadn't been an empty invitation.

"I'm ready whenever you are," Rhonda said, once she came out of the bedroom. "You have to know I don't like imposing on you and Francine."

"Did we ever say anything about you being an imposition? I even promised Francine I'd take all of us out to dinner tonight. Now come on, if we keep her waiting, she won't be a happy camper."

~ * ~

Rhonda found Bob's guest room to be very comfortable and Francine a very gracious hostess. Mark checked in with her and it took a lot of talking to convince him to stay in Las Vegas until Sunday morning when his original flight was scheduled.

The morning after Rhonda's move to Bob's house, she sat in her office waiting for Geri Salizar to arrive for her appointment at eleven thirty. She'd seen Geri at the campgrounds as well as at the funeral, but the woman who entered the office was definitely an entirely different Geri than Rhonda saw before.

At the campgrounds, Geri wore tight Daisy Dukes as well as a belly shirt that showed off her diamond studded belly ring. At the funeral, she wore a very tight as well as revealing black dress. Today she was dressed in a red print sundress with a white eyelet jacket.

"Thank you for coming in," Rhonda said, once Geri was seated. "We have a few more questions we want to ask you."

Geri looked apprehensive but nodded her understanding.

"We met with Pete's friends from Madison, and they told us about some college kids who were harassing the people at the club. Did you know about it?"

"Not at the time. I had a bad case of the creeping crud the night Pete went to the club alone. He came over to see if I would go with him, but I had to beg off. My head was aching so bad I thought it was going to explode."

"He told you about it, though?"

"Eventually, but I practically had to pull it out of him. For about three weeks, he always seemed to have an excuse on 'our' night to go to the club. I finally asked him what was going on and he told me about it. He said there'd been a bunch of kids from the University who came to the club to cause trouble. Most of them were nothing more than curious teenagers, but a couple of them were outwardly gay. Before they left, they said some terrible things, and I think Pete took them to heart. It really crushed him, if you know what I mean."

"Did Pete know who these kids were?"

"Not that I know of. When we finally went back to Madison, he was paranoid every time the door opened, and someone came in. It took a couple of weeks before he was comfortable again."

"From what we learned in Madison, these guys were verbally abusive. It seems like they were totally against the lifestyle."

"That's the impression I got from Pete. Of course, the others wouldn't even talk about it. It must have been a bad scene. I've never known any of them to be as spooked as they were after it happened."

"Can you tell me when it was?" Rhonda knew the answer but wanted confirmation from Geri.

"The week I couldn't go to Madison was the second week in May. I thought it was just college kids out for kicks, but Pete saw it differently."

Once Geri left the office, Bob looked at Rhonda with a knowing look in his eyes. "I have a feeling we've got our connection between Pete and Brandon."

"I think you're right. Our killer saw Pete as a freak of nature. Since he wasn't straight or completely gay, being a transvestite wasn't acceptable. As for Brandon, if he really was a homophobe, the killer would have seen him as a threat. Whoever this guy is, he's local and that means he could strike again at any time."

"Come on, Rhonda, he already has. I'm afraid that brick through your window wasn't just a prank. It was a verified warning. I had a talk with Sheriff Cantwell this morning and he agrees with me that until this nightmare is over, you and Mark will have protection at the house."

Rhonda rolled her eyes. The last thing she wanted was to have someone else in her home, even if it was for her own good.

~ * ~

"I just got back the lab report on the note that came through your window with that brick," Bob said later that afternoon.

Rhonda wondered why the lab would send the report to Bob when it was her window that was shattered by the brick. The thought no more than crossed her mind when she realized she was the victim and not the officer of record for this one. Besides, the lab was giving them the courtesy of getting the report to them. Technically, the officer of record was the responding officer from the city.

"What does it say?"

"Either our guy is getting careless, or he knows we can't trace his fingerprints. They lifted a good one from the paper but couldn't get a match."

Rhonda sighed. These weren't the results she wanted to hear. In a perfect world, they would have lifted a print and matched it immediately. What she didn't want to admit was they lived in a very imperfect world.

Chapter Thirteen

"I certainly didn't need you to come to the bus station with me," Rhonda complained to Bob as they waited for Mark's bus to arrive from O'Hare.

"You know, as well as I do, I'm here under orders from Sheriff Cantwell."

"Well, it's still ridiculous. We haven't heard anything from the murderer since the note was thrown through my window. It's one thing for someone to commit vandalism, it's another to try and kill a cop."

Rather than continue to vent her frustration, Rhonda kicked at the curb. She knew both Bob and Sheriff Cantwell were right, but she didn't like to be accompanied everywhere she went.

The sound of an approaching vehicle preceded the aroma of diesel fuel as the bus from Chicago pulled into the first parking slot. She watched as several people got off before Mark came down the steps.

All thoughts of the injustice of being under guard left her mind as she hurried to embrace her husband. They'd been separated before, but the stress of this time was almost more than she could stand.

"I wasn't gone that long, honey," Mark whispered in her ear.

"It seemed like forever."

Once they broke their embrace, Mark turned toward Bob. "It's good to see you, Bob. Something tells me you aren't here meeting someone coming in on the bus."

"You're right. When your house was vandalized, there was a note attached to the brick. In it, Rhonda was threatened. I'm along for protection and there will be an officer at your house until this thing is over."

"What if this doesn't get over? What if the two of you don't solve this?"

"Don't even talk like that, Mark," Rhonda pleaded. "We've gotten a couple of leads. We just have to put two and two together and hope it doesn't add up to five."

Before either of the men could reply, Bob's cell phone rang. Rhonda watched his expression as he answered. The worry lines across his forehead didn't bode well for how the rest of this evening was going to go.

"I'm sorry about this, but you'll have to call a cab, Mark. That was Sheriff Cantwell on the phone. There's been another incident. We need to investigate."

"W-where?" Rhonda stammered.

The look in Bob's eyes told her it wasn't anything he wanted to discuss in front of Mark.

"It's okay, honey," Mark assured her. "I know when duty calls you have to answer. I saw Jim Lamont on the bus. If I hurry, I can catch a ride to the house with him. I will be able to get into the house, won't I?"

"We'll call the officer on duty and advise him you'll be alone," Bob said as he shook Mark's hand.

Reluctantly, Rhonda followed Bob to where he'd parked his vehicle. "Now, where are we going?"

"We've been called to the hospital. It seems as though David Olson was assaulted when he got out of his car."

Rhonda thought of the man voted most unlikely to succeed from the class reunion, as well as his wife Marcie, the talented lawyer. "Oh, my dear lord, is he all right?"

"Sheriff Cantwell says he's pretty banged up, but he's conscious. Marcy is there with him."

"What makes Cantwell think this might be related to our case?"

"When Marcy heard the commotion, she ran outside. There was a note beside David's body, but the assailants were gone."

Rhonda took a deep breath. She had no love for Marcy, but David was a different matter. She'd never met a gentler person in her life. Even though she couldn't imagine meek David and overbearing Marcy as a couple, they both assured her they had an undying love.

By the time they got to the hospital, David had already been admitted to ICU. Marcy sat at his bedside, her makeup smudged and tears washing her cheeks.

"Oh, Rhonda, I'm so glad you're the one they sent," Marcy gushed before there was another onset of tears. "Jackson and Cindy have only good things to say about you."

The compliment caught Rhonda off guard. That connected with the crack in the façade Marcy usually portrayed to show Rhonda the real Marcy.

"Can you tell us what happened?"

Marcy shook her head as more tears seemed to cut off her words.

"Weren't you with David when he came home tonight?"

Marcy sniffed loudly. "Sunday night is our special night. I usually get all dressed up in something sexy, toss a salad and chill the wine while David goes out to get us a pizza at Morelli's. It's our favorite place. I was in the kitchen. I didn't hear anything until I decided it was past time for David to come back. I went to the front of the house and could hear shouting. By the time I got outside, David was lying in the driveway in a pool of blood. I just caught a glimpse of an old truck pulling around the corner. I couldn't even begin to give you description."

"I have to ask these questions, Marcy," Rhonda began.

"I know you do. The only thing I remember is seeing a piece of white paper on the ground next to David."

"What did it say?"

Marcy's head came up suddenly to meet Rhonda eye to eye. Rather than the wife of the victim, the hardnosed lawyer returned.

"I know better than to touch evidence. We have a rock garden next to the driveway. I took one of the larger rocks and put it on top of the note before I went into the house to get my cell phone. Once I had it, I came out to sit beside David and I called 911."

"You did the right thing. Do you have any idea why anyone would attack David?"

Marcy turned to give David a loving look and again her demeanor changed. "I can't think of one person who would want to harm him. He's the most giving and loving man I've ever met."

Rhonda heard Bob's cell phone ring and looked up in time to see him step out into the hall for privacy.

"You said something earlier I didn't understand. How close are you to Jackson and Cindy Hayes?"

"You have to know David and I went to school with Jackson. David's parents owned the farm next to theirs."

"Farm? Isn't there a subdivision next to the Hayes farm?"

"There is now, but when we were in high school, David's parents owned that land. His dad was killed in a farm accident when we were sophomores in high school. Shortly after that, my mom died of cancer and my dad was killed in a car accident. David's mother, Anna May, was such a wonderful woman. When she found out I was completely alone, she went to social services and became my legal guardian. I guess that was when I fell in love with David and the rest, as they say, is history."

Marcy smiled and looked lovingly at David. "Of course, that's not what you were asking about, was it, Rhonda? David and Jackson grew up together. They were the best of friends, still are. When we were first married, Jackson's one night off from milking every week was Saturday. Once a month Jackson, Cindy, David, and I would get together to play cards. It gave David and Cindy a chance to show off their cooking abilities."

"David and Cindy?" Rhonda interrupted.

"With me going to school and working so hard, David took over all the household duties. He's actually a gourmet cook. It's a good thing, too, since I can burn water. If we had to live off my cooking, I'm afraid we'd all starve to death." Rhonda made notes furiously as Marcy continued.

"David's mother was gone by then and we decided to rent out the farmland. The money we got from that, combined with my scholarships and inheritance, allowed me to go to school and David to stay at home with the kids. We both got exactly what we wanted out of life. I don't know if I could go on without him."

"Did you know Jackson's kids?"

"What a silly question. Neither of us could afford a sitter, so when we got together the kids were included."

"Rhonda," Bob called from the doorway. "Can you come out here for a minute?"

Rhonda excused herself and went to join Bob in the hall. "What did Sheriff Cantwell have to say?"

"More than you want to know. We need to get out of here and go to your place."

"My place? Why? Has something happened to Mark?"

"Mark's fine. He's the one who called in the report. I'll fill you in on the way."

"I need to go in and talk to Marcy. I'll meet you at the car." Rhonda turned to go back into the cubicle where David lay unconscious.

"I have to leave for a while," she said. As soon as the word passed her lips, Rhonda saw a look of despair in Marcy's eyes.

"What if David comes to? Who will take his statement?"

"I promise I'll be back. There's something I have to take care of. While I'm gone, I'll make certain there's a guard at the door."

In an action that seemed completely out of character for Marcy, she held out her hand to Rhonda. Rather than a traditional handshake, she squeezed Rhonda's hand and nodded her head.

"Thank you, Rhonda. Thank you so much for being here for us."

~ * ~

Bob waited in the car for her with the air conditioning cranked against the heat of the late August evening.

"Now, what's going on?" Rhonda demanded.

"When Mark got home there was some vandalism to your back yard and a note taped to your grill on the deck. Sheriff Cantwell is there with Mark, and I told him we'd get there as soon as possible."

"Are you sure Mark isn't hurt?"

"Positive. The damage was already done when he got home this evening."

Every possible scenario ran through Rhonda's mind as Bob maneuvered the streets between the hospital and the house she shared with Mark. She thanked God Mark was out of town for the past few days. At least he'd been spared the frustrations she'd been feeling over this investigation as well as the horror of being targeted by what was turning into a serial killer.

The flashing of lights of police cars lining the street leading to her house greeted Rhonda. One vehicle had the words 'SWAT TEAM' stenciled on the door, making her heart pound faster in anticipation. Any thoughts of being a trained officer drained from her being as she became the victim for the second time in a week.

"Why would the SWAT TEAM be here?" she questioned.

"Sheriff Cantwell told me they were checking your house since the patio door was smashed. They are sweeping the house to make certain there's no one inside."

Rhonda nodded. *Of course, that's what they're doing. If I was thinking right, I wouldn't be questioning this.*

In front of the house, she saw Mark talking to Sheriff Cantwell. It was a relief to see the two of them together, but the reason behind their conversation was frightening.

"Are you alright?" she asked once she joined the two of them.

"I'm fine. I haven't even been in the house, since I didn't know what I'd find."

"How bad is it?"

Mark took her in his arms. "Not as bad as it could have been if you were here when they came. The patio door is broken, and the furniture is tossed around on the deck. They ripped up a couple of plants in the backyard and taped a note to the hood of the grill."

"What did the note say?"

"We don't know yet," Sheriff Cantwell said, answering her question. "We sent it directly to the lab. With all these notes they're working a lot of overtime this weekend."

"House is clear," the officer who came around from the back said. "As far as I can tell, there is no damage inside. It's like once they smashed in the patio door, they left without going in. Would you like to go in with your husband, Detective Pohs, and make certain everything is alright?"

Mark squeezed her hand. "I'll be right by your side, honey," he said. "We can go in and look around, but I doubt we can stay here tonight."

All of a sudden, Rhonda thought of the officer who was supposed to be assigned at the house. "Where was the officer who was going to be staying here?"

Cantwell looked as perplexed at the question as Rhonda felt. It was the officer from the city who sheepishly answered. "Well, we were told you wouldn't be here until after you picked your husband up from the bus station. We thought it would be all right not to send anyone over until after seven when we knew you'd both be here. Of course, we got the call from Mr. Pohs around six and all of our plans changed."

Anger welled deep in Rhonda's gut. "I was told someone would be here twenty-four/seven from the time I left to stay at my partner's home. I'd say someone dropped the ball here. Do you have any idea when this vandalism took place?"

"Not really, but looking at your backyard, I can understand why the neighbors didn't report anything. This is a pretty secluded area considering you're in the city."

"That doesn't excuse…"

"We know it doesn't. We dropped the ball, but what is past is past. We can't change it, just move on and…"

Sheriff Cantwell interrupted the officer. "Don't give me that crap. I need to talk to your chief right now. This is unacceptable. Detective Pohs was supposed to have around the clock protection…"

Rhonda didn't stay to listen to the remainder of Cantwell's rant. Instead, Mark led her toward the front door and used his key to let them in.

"It's good to be home," he said, taking her in his arms, away from prying eyes for the first time since his return.

"I'm so sorry about all this mess. It should have never invaded our personal space."

"It certainly did. Guess that's all part of being married to the top detective for the county. Are you going to miss all of this?"

Rhonda thought for a minute before answering. "I'll miss the people and maybe the job, but not the drama. I think this will be a good move for us, even if I'm not able to work in law enforcement. Who knows, maybe I'll get a job dealing blackjack in one of the casinos on the strip."

"That will be the day. I did find us a place to rent. It's outside of town, but the owner lives here. From what I hear, she got it as part of her divorce settlement and hasn't been able to sell it. I'm going to talk to her next week. If we like living there, hopefully, she'll be receptive to working out a good price for us."

Thoughts of the upcoming move to Vegas ran through Rhonda's mind as she checked out the house to see if anything was missing. Relief overshadowed anticipation when she realized nothing inside had been disturbed. What damage was done was on the outside. It was nothing that couldn't be repaired. Unfortunately, security was no longer intact.

~ * ~

"I have the contents of the two notes," Bob greeted them when they rejoined him on the front porch.

"I'll leave the two of you alone," Mark said. "I'll go in and pack us a bag, since we can't stay here tonight."

Once Mark returned to the house, Rhonda turned to face Bob. "Give me the bad news."

"Since we think the damage was done to your place before David was attacked, I'll give you yours first. It reads:

THE END IS NEAR – SORRY YOU WEREN'T HOME SO I COULD DELIVER MY MESSAGE PERSONALLY."

Rhonda inhaled deeply. "What does the one left at the Olson's place say?"

"YOU ARE THE ALPHA AND THE OMEGA."

"The beginning and the end," Rhonda mused. "I wonder what that means and how it's all connected to the other two murders. If David doesn't survive this, we're looking at a third murder. Whoever this guy is, he's turned into a serial killer."

"He most certainly has. That's why Francine insists I bring you and Mark back to our place tonight."

"I don't think we should. It would be putting you and Francine in danger. I don't want something like that on my conscience if something were to happen."

"Don't worry about it. After Cantwell read the city Chief of Police the riot act, he called in the state boys. Our place will be well guarded."

Chapter Fourteen

"We're supposed to work from home today," Bob announced at breakfast.

"Just what can we do from here?" Rhonda protested.

"Don't ask me. I'm just following orders. Face it Rhonda, you and Mark have been warned not once but twice. Can't you get it through your head your life is in danger?"

Rhonda picked up a piece of toast but put it back down on her plate without even tasting it. "I have a feeling David Olson was the last name on the list. The note said David was the beginning and the end. I think the threats were to get me off the case. If this is the end of it, he thinks he's home free. He can disappear and leave us with several unsolved cases."

Bob's cell phone rang, ending the conversation. After he left the kitchen to take the call, Rhonda returned her attention to breakfast.

"We really appreciate you putting up with us, Francine," Mark commented.

"Nonsense," Francine replied. "I've enjoyed playing hostess. With Bob's job, we don't get to entertain as much as I'd like."

Bob returned to the kitchen. "Guess we won't be stuck here after all. Cantwell is sending over bodyguards to take us to the hospital. David has regained consciousness." Rhonda quickly finished her breakfast and went back to the guest room to dress for the day. To her surprise, Mark followed closely behind.

"I worry about you going out today," Mark said, once they were alone in the bedroom.

"I wish you wouldn't worry. I'll be well protected."

"I hope so. When this case is over, I want to take you out to Las Vegas so you can see the place I want to rent for us. I'm planning to talk to the woman who owns it today. I think you're going to love it."

"You know I will. If it's something you're this excited about, it has to be special. I hope that with David regaining consciousness, he'll remember something to end this case."

~ * ~

Although she understood the need for protection, Rhonda resented the two county deputies assigned to take them from Bob's house to the hospital.

They met Marcy and Jackson Hayes in the waiting room. Just looking at Marcy, Rhonda knew the woman hadn't left the hospital since David's attack.

"We heard David regained consciousness," Rhonda said as soon as they entered the room.

"He came to this morning, he's very disoriented. The doctors are in with him now. That's why we were kicked out." Marcy glanced at Jackson. "I don't know what I would have done if Cindy hadn't dropped Jackson off last night. We're blessed to have such wonderful friends."

"You knew we'd be here for you and David," Jackson commented. "Hopefully this will give you a break in these cases. Somehow, I think all this shit will end up being traced back to one person."

Rhonda agreed. Before she could comment, a nurse came into the room. "You and Mr. Hayes can go in now, Mrs. Olson."

"When can we talk to Mr. Olson?" Bob asked, flashing his badge.

"Let them go in first, Marcy," Jackson suggested. "You've been here all night. I'll take you out to our place so you can catch a nap and a shower. I'm sure anything Cindy has in her closet will fit you perfectly."

Exhaustion was reflected on Marcy's face as she nodded her agreement. Rhonda watched them leave before turning to follow the nurse back to the ICU area.

The monitors still beeped softly in David's cubicle. Although he lay perfectly still, Rhonda did notice his eyes were open.

"David," she began, "do you remember me, Detective Pohs?"

Slowly, David nodded his head.

"This is my partner, Detective Masters. Can you tell us what happened to you?"

The trach tube attached to David's throat prevented him from speaking, but he motioned for the pen and pad of paper on the night table next to the bed.

Attacked he wrote.

"Do you know who it was?"

From behind.

Bob asked several more questions, but David's confusion clouded receiving answers that would have made any sense. As they left the ICU area, one of the nurses approached them.

"I don't know if this makes any sense, but when Mr. Olson first came to he was very agitated. We'd sent his wife down to the coffee shop, so I asked him if there was something I could get for him. He motioned he wanted a pad and pen. This is what he wrote."

Rhonda took the paper and studied the writing. Had she not known better, she would have sworn an aged person had written it.

GAR

"Can we keep this?" Bob asked.

"Most certainly. I made a copy of it to put in his file. Dr. Bradshaw said we should ask his wife about it but by the time I talked to him she was in the waiting room, and I was busy with another patient."

Bob thanked the nurse, taking note of her name 'Susan' from her name tag.

"Interesting," he said, as they made their way back to the two deputies waiting for them just outside the ICU area. "Any guess what GAR could mean?"

Rhonda shook her head, bewildered. "It could be anything from a name to an acronym. It has to mean something though, or it wouldn't have been the first thing he wrote."

"It would be a lot easier if he could talk to us. Maybe we should stop at the Olson house and see if Marcy can shed some light on its meaning."

"We wouldn't find her there. Don't you remember she went out to the Hayes farm with Jackson?"

"That's right. Doesn't that seem a little off to you? Why would Jackson stay here while Cindy went back out to the farm? Wouldn't you think he would be the one to go back home while Cindy stayed to console Marcy?"

"Last night when you were taking the call from Sheriff Cantwell, I had some time alone with Marcy. I have a feeling she's not as close to Cindy as David is to Jackson. They've been friends since they were little kids together. I guess I can understand Jackson wanting to be here."

"Then I guess we'll be making a trip out to the Hayes farm. By now, I bet you can make that trip with your eyes closed."

Chapter Fifteen

For the first time, Rhonda saw the Hayes' farm as a peaceful rural setting. Even though they were riding in a squad car, there were no flashing lights or emergency vehicles filling the dooryard.

They were hardly out of the car when Cindy Hayes came out to meet them. "Is there any news on Brandon's killer?" she questioned, the words tumbling over themselves and mingled with tears.

"I'm sorry Mrs. Hayes," Bob said moving to face the woman before Rhonda could get out of the car, "We were told Marcy Olson is here."

"Oh yes, I insisted Jackson bring her back here so she could rest. The goings on the past few weeks have taken a toll on us all."

Rhonda wondered about the sincerity of Cindy's words, just as she'd questioned Jackson's concern for Marcy at the hospital. Was she reading too much into their friendship, or was there something going on between Jackson and Marcy? In no way could Cindy begin to compete with Marcy's good looks, and it was the same between Jackson and David.

Cindy gestured toward the house, leading the way up the steps to the veranda style front porch. Rhonda hardly finished climbing the steps when Marcy hurried out to greet them.

"It's David, isn't it? I knew I shouldn't let Jackson talk me into leaving the hospital. I knew it, I just knew it."

"David's doing well," Ronda said, hoping to reassure Marcy. "When we left the hospital, he was sleeping. We're here because of something he wrote when he first woke up. Do these letters mean anything to you?"

Bob handed Marcy the note. Jackson joined the women on the porch and the three of them looked at it intently.

"I don't understand what this could mean," Jackson said before either of the women could answer.

Rhonda studied the three people in front of her, assessing their reaction. Somehow, she knew those three letters had a meaning, but she had no idea what it could be.

"Are you sure?" Bob pressed.

"Well," Marcy replied, drawing out the word, making it seem as though it lasted several seconds. "Maybe he meant to write Gary. He's our oldest. With all the excitement, I haven't had time to call the kids."

"Where are your kids?" Bob inquired.

Marcy hesitated for a moment. "Gary goes to school at UW in Madison. During the school year, he had a job up there as well, but I don't know what he's been doing this summer. You know how it is with adult kids. They don't always keep in touch with the old people. Allison is our daughter and she's in the military and stationed in Alaska. I didn't want to contact either of them before I knew what was happening with David.

"I understand perfectly," Bob said, flashing Rhonda a look that warned her to hold her tongue. "I'm sorry we frightened you. We'll be in touch."

With a nod of his head, Bob led the way back to the waiting cruiser. "What do you mean you understand?" Rhonda asked after they pulled back onto the highway. "They're all holding something back."

"Of course, they are. I doubt the first person David would think of would be the son Marcy hasn't even contacted.

"I hear you there. I don't have kids, but if I did and something like this happened to Mark, you can bet I'd be calling them right away."

Bob nodded. "I think we need to find out more about Gary Olson."

~ * ~

"What do you know about a kid named Gary Olson, Mark?" Bob asked once they were back at the house.

Mark wrinkled his brow as if trying to place the name. "He wasn't into sports, but I remember hearing about him. If I were to see a picture of him in the yearbook that might help jog my memory."

"Do you think you can get one for us?" Rhonda inquired.

"I can do better than that. If you know when this kid graduated, I could pull it up on the Internet. That has been the big project for the computer club for the last few years. They set up a website and uploaded the senior pictures of all the classes. It's been an ongoing project. The last I heard, they had everything loaded back to the 1970's. They're planning to go all the way back to when the school was founded in the 1920's."

Rhonda felt a rush of excitement. She knew it had been a long shot that Gary Olson actually went to school in town. The Olson's home was relatively new, meaning the kid could have gone to school in Clinton before the move. She thanked God Mark remembered the name.

It took only a matter of minutes for Mark to bring up the yearbook website. After going back several years, they were looking at a picture of Gary.

The boy in the photo was almost too pretty to be male. Marcy's good looks mingled well with David's small stature and chiseled features.

"Is there any way we can send a copy of this picture to the printer?" Rhonda asked.

Mark looked up at her, a smile crossing his lips. Even though his primary duties at the school were in the athletic department, he was a computer geek in his own right.

"That's not a problem," Mark replied, clicking several buttons to isolate the picture they needed copied. "How many do you want me to run?"

Rhonda and Bob exchanged glances, trying to decide what they would need. "I'd say at least four. I'd like to drop one off with Sheriff Cantwell, have one for the file on this case and one each for Bob and myself."

The printer made a grinding sound as almost instantly the first copy of the picture came out, followed by three more. Once the printing was complete, Mark and Francine left Bob and Rhonda alone while they went over the changing aspects of this complicated case.

"First we have Pete Potter's murder," Rhonda began. "We know he's a cross-dresser who goes to the clubs in Madison where he was harassed by several gay college students. He's also a skirt chaser and came on to every woman at the reunion. After his murder, we found the first note at his house."

Bob jotted notes on a legal pad. "That's when you decided it wasn't any of the women he pissed off at the reunion. Right after we found that note, the Hayes kid was killed, and we got the second one. Finally, you got the third note while Mark was out in Las Vegas. Thank goodness all that happened to you was vandalism rather than murder."

"I'm sure the note Mark found at the house was left while I was staying here. So far, the last note is the one we found at the Olson home after David was attacked."

Bob nodded his head. "I agree with you. The problem is, how do we connect the dots?"

Rhonda contemplated her answer. "I tend to side with Marcy. I think David was trying to write Gary, his son's name. Do you think it was because he wanted to see his son or because his son was the one who attacked him?"

"I don't know about that. Why would this kid attack his own father and kill two others, to say nothing of threatening you?"

"You pose a good question. I don't think we'll get any answers until we can talk to Gary, if we can talk to him. Did you see the reaction of Marcy as well as Jackson and Cindy Hayes when they talked about him? Something's not right about this guy. I just can't put my finger on it."

Rhonda momentarily reviewed the contents of the five notes left at various locations. In doing so, she tried to make sense of the messages as a whole, rather than taking each of them individually.

"I think we need to go back to the hospital and meet with David again," Bob suggested. "If we're lucky he's breathing without the ventilator and will be able to talk to us."

As much as Rhonda wanted to go to the hospital on their own, she patiently waited while Bob called dispatch and asked to have two deputies come to the house and pick them up.

~ * ~

Rhonda and Bob stopped at the ICU waiting room to call the nurses' station to see if they could visit David. To their disappointment, they were told he was sleeping and not to be disturbed.

"Where to now?" Bob asked, once they were back in the squad car where the two deputies waited for them.

"I think we should go back to your place and regroup," Rhonda said, winking at Bob in the hopes he would realize she wanted to shake their watch dogs.

"Good idea. Hopefully, we can get a lead on where to find Gary Olson."

"Do you mean Gary-The-Fairy?" the younger of the two deputies asked.

"What do you mean by that?" Bob questioned.

"I didn't mean any disrespect, but Gary Olson transferred to our high school at the beginning of his freshman year. I was a senior and well, everyone knew he was different. As soon as he came, we gave him that nickname."

"Are you saying Gary is gay?" Rhonda inquired.

"I guess I am. I thought everyone knew about him. He was smart, my brother was in his class, and he graduated with honors. The last I heard he was on the dean's list at UW. You've got to have a lot on the ball to get that kind of an honor."

Rhonda and Bob exchanged glances. She hoped he was thinking the same thing as she. All of a sudden, the last note made sense.

If Gary was gay, it was only natural for him to blame his father for the way he'd turned out. It also explained Pete's murder. The people they'd talked to in Madison said there were some gay college students who harassed Pete at the club. It was entirely possible he had some kind of grudge against the man who'd known his parents since high school. What didn't make sense was the murder of Brandon Hayes. Of course, the vandalism and notes at her house probably meant nothing more than the frustration he felt over her investigating the case.

"If you need us again," the younger of the two officers said once they arrived at Bob's house, "just give dispatch a call and we'll be glad to come back."

Bob thanked them and hurried inside with Rhonda. "I take it you picked up on what that kid said about Gary being gay."

"I certainly did," she replied. "I think we should call Patrick and Mike and find out if they have either a fax machine or an e-mail where we can send Gary's picture. Something tells me they're going to confirm Gary is the kid who was harassing them in the club."

"I do too. Why don't you give Patrick a call and see if he can give us the information for both of them."

Rhonda was glad both Mark and Francine were out of the house. She knew Mark was meeting with the owner of the house in Las Vegas and Bob told her Francine was meeting her sister for coffee at Starbucks.

Rhonda found Patrick's number stored in her phone. She was relieved when he answered on the first ring.

"Is there something I can help you with, Detective?" he asked as soon as the connection was complete.

"I hope so. When we met the other day, you talked about some gay men who were bothering you at the club. Would you recognize one of them if we were to send you a picture?"

"I'm pretty sure I would, but if I couldn't I know Mike could. He and Pete got up close and personal with them while I was at the bar getting a drink."

"What about Geri?" Rhonda asked, testing the waters. It wasn't like she didn't believe Geri's story, but it was always best to double check things like this.

"As I recall, she wasn't there that night. Pete said she was sick with the bug that was hitting everyone hard. Of course, there were a lot of times when Pete would call and say he was coming up alone. She was a lot of fun, but sometimes it was best if it was just us guys, if you get my drift."

Rhonda talked for a few minutes more making note of the e-mail addresses for both Patrick and Mike. As soon as she hung up, Bob scanned the photo into the computer, and they sent the two e-mails.

"Now it's just a cat and mouse game waiting for a response from these guys," he said after hitting the send button.

"Maybe while we're waiting, we could contact the UW and find out if they have an address for Gary Olson."

"Do you think they keep track of things like that?" Bob questioned.

"I don't know, but anything is worth a shot. I got the impression Marcy wasn't too anxious to talk about her oldest son. I also think there's something more going on between the Hayes and Olson families than we see on the surface."

"What do you mean?"

"Friends are friends, but Jackson seems to be overly protective of Marcy. It wouldn't surprise me if those four are more than just friends. I'm not naïve enough that I haven't heard of wife swapping or swinging. There could be something like that going on."

Bob laughed at her assumption. "I think you read too many books. You haven't moved to Las Vegas yet. This is Wisconsin for god's sake. Life here is pretty tame."

Rhonda laughed at Bob's statement. "I certainly didn't take you for an ostrich. I think it's time to get your head out of the sand. Ever since the sexual revolution over fifty years ago people have been doing it with someone other than their spouses."

"I don't agree. Jackson and Cindy are good friends and nothing more. Those two couples are so straight laced, I bet the women don't fart and the guys don't scratch their balls."

"They're the ones you have to watch out for. You know what they say about still waters running deep. It seems to me there was a lot of that kind of thing going on when I was a kid. The parents of some of my friends belonged to a swinger's club. I can't believe it would all come to a screeching halt. It's just too much fun for some people."

Bob stared at her, slack jawed, until her phone rang just as the computer indicated a new e-mail had been received in Bob's inbox.

"Pohs here," she answered.

"I'm sending a squad over to pick the two of you up," Sheriff Cantwell greeted her. "There's been a change in David Olson's condition. I want you over at the hospital immediately. It might be your last chance to get any information from him."

Rhonda looked at Bob and then at the computer screen. The inbox showed e-mails from both Patrick and Mike. Before saying anything, Rhonda watched as Bob opened both of them. The messages were both the same. Gary Olson was one of the young men who they'd seen at the club.

"We have to get to the hospital," she said, once they finished reading the messages. "Cantwell is sending over a squad for us."

Rhonda's heart pounded as she quickly jotted a note to Mark telling him where they were. If David's condition had taken a turn for the worse, it could be too late by the time they could make it to the hospital.

Chapter Sixteen

After instructing the deputies to wait for them in the lobby, Rhonda and Bob went straight up to ICU without stopping at the desk.

In the ICU waiting room, they found Marcy being comforted by both Jackson and Cindy Hayes.

"He's gone," Jackson said, holding Marcy in a comforting embrace. "We got here about fifteen minutes ago and everything seemed to be going well. That was when he had a seizure. Before we knew it, he stopped breathing. The doctors worked on him, but they said there was nothing they could do. They think a blood clot broke loose and went into his brain causing a massive stroke."

Rhonda took a deep breath. "I'm so sorry, Marcy. Did you ever reach your kids?"

Marcy nodded. "I talked to Allison right after the two of you left the farm. She's getting emergency leave and coming home. Gary, well, he's not answering his cell phone. I called his roommates, and they told me he moved out this summer. They haven't heard from him since school let out in June. He told them he was going to be doing some backpacking. No one seems to know where he is."

"Is that unusual?" Bob asked.

"Not really. Gary is an adult. Quite often we don't hear from him for long periods of time. He's been on his own ever since he graduated from high school. As long as I keep signing the checks for his tuition and spending money, he's happy with his life at the University. He's studying to be an architect."

Rhonda looked up at Bob, questioning the strange parent-child relationship Marcy was describing.

"Can we talk to you, Mrs. Olson?" a doctor said as he entered the waiting room.

"Whatever you have to say can be said in front of my friends," Marcy replied.

"We need to have you sign the forms so we can do the autopsy."

Marcy's knees buckled as she collapsed into Jackson's arms. "Oh no, this can't be happening. Do you have to cut him open?"

"It's standard procedure in cases like this," Bob commented. "There's an ongoing investigation going on about your husband's assault. We need to find out if the blood clot was as a result of the beating he took or something that couldn't have been predicted. If it is from the assault, the charge goes to murder. If not, I don't want to be making false accusations against whoever did this."

"Detective Masters is right, Marcy," Jackson agreed. "We need to know what actually caused David's death."

Marcy nodded and allowed Jackson to take her out of the room to the office where the doctor said she'd be able to sign the necessary papers. Once they were gone, Rhonda turned her attention to Cindy.

"I'm very sorry for your loss. It seems as though the four of you were close friends."

"Yes we were. Jackson and David were best friends all through school. Jackson was David's best friend and David was at our wedding as well. Of course, Marcy and Jackson were close as well. They were all a group in high school and…"

"…and what, Cindy?"

"Ah…nothing."

"It must be something or you wouldn't have mentioned it."

"Is there something I can help you with?" Jackson asked, coming into the room.

"Cindy was telling us about your relationship with Marcy and David," Bob replied. "Is it possible there was more to it than just friendship?"

"You have a filthy mind, Detective. This is neither the time nor the place for any questions like this. Marcy just lost her husband and Cindy, and I just lost our best friend. We have to make arrangements for the service for the gentlest man in the world. If you'll excuse me, I'm taking my wife and Marcy home."

Jackson ushered the two women from the room, leaving Rhonda and Bob alone.

"Well," Rhonda began, "that was different. I think we're onto something about the relationship between those two families."

"I tend to agree. For now, I want to talk to the doctor who was treating David. Hopefully he can shed some light on what just happened."

Together they crossed the hall to the office where Marcy went to sign the papers authorizing the autopsy.

"Can we talk to you, Doctor?" Bob asked.

The man looked up. "Of course, Detective, what can I help you with?"

"You said David Olson died of a stroke. Is there a possibility it was something that would have happened without the beating he endured?"

"I doubt it. I checked his medical records. He just had a physical last month and he's healthier than most men his age. There were no signs of high blood pressure or any other problems that would trigger a stroke. From what I've learned about my patient, he led a very stress-free life. We should all be so lucky."

Rhonda waited until they were alone in the elevator before commenting on what the doctor just said. "I wonder just how stress-free David's life was."

"What do you mean?"

"You're a man. How would you feel if Francine was the one supporting your family? Would you be content to be a house husband? How would you have felt about staying home and taking care of the kids, knowing your wife was superior to you, not only because she was the main breadwinner, but her intelligence surpassed yours as well?"

"I see what you mean. In my class we had a kid like David. We all made fun of him because we were mean teenagers. His name was Zack Dorinski. The last I heard of him, he was working for a factory down by Rockton and he'd married the daughter of one of the professors at UW Whitewater. I haven't thought about him in years. He's just one of those forgettable characters that cross your path in life."

"Right, and David would have been someone like that if he hadn't married Marcy. I can remember the mother of one of my friends saying she wished she knew what her real identity was. All her life she'd been her parents' daughter, her husband's wife, and her kid's mother, she never stood out for anything on her own."

Chapter Seventeen

With the mess of the break-in cleaned up, Rhonda and Mark returned to their own house. As a precaution, they'd installed a security system. Rhonda found it a pain to have to disarm it every time she came home, but agreed with Mark it was a necessary evil.

On the morning of the visitation for David Olson, Rhonda went with Mark to meet with Dawn, the woman who owned the house he'd found in Las Vegas. They met her at a local coffee shop, and she brought with her pictures of the home she now owned but never wanted to live in again.

"Will you both be working in Las Vegas?" she asked.

"I'll be working at one of the prep schools out there," Mark replied. "Unfortunately, my beautiful wife has yet to hear back from any of the law enforcement agencies in the area."

"Well, that shouldn't be a problem," Dawn quipped. "I've been reading about you in the papers ever since you first started solving murders. I do have some connections out there. I'd be happy to put in a good word for you."

"How long have you owned the house?" Rhonda inquired.

"My ex-husband and I bought it about ten years ago. I thought we'd retire out there, but about four years ago everything changed. He started going to the casino more than usual. I found out he was dating one of the dealers. When we got back to Wisconsin, I filed for divorce. In the settlement I got the Las Vegas house and very little else. He married his little sweetie last year at Christmas and promptly cut my support down to almost nil."

Rhonda felt sorry for Dawn. She saw too many women in the same situation and thanked her lucky stars Mark wasn't the kind of man who lusted after other women.

As she looked at the pictures of Dawn's house, she realized it had been decorated with a discerning eye. She could almost see Dawn selecting the furniture as well as the wall decorations that would grace the rooms of the house where she planned to retire. Now all of it had changed and she was anxious to have someone living in the house and possibly buy it from her.

"What do you think, honey?" Mark asked.

"If we can afford it, I think we should take it. It looks like it would be perfect for us."

"The way it sounds, I guess we have a deal, Dawn. I have a check for the security. I have to be in Las Vegas by the end of October. When Rhonda can join me will depend on how quickly she can finish up with this case she's working on, get our house on the market and sold."

Rhonda thought about having Mark go out to Las Vegas without her. The way this case was going, it was entirely possible she could spend many months either trying to sell the house or solve her current case while he settled into the beautiful home they had just agreed to rent.

~ * ~

Rhonda and Bob went through the line to pay their respects to David's family. Beside Marcy, stood a couple, both in uniform. Rhonda knew it had to be Allison and her husband from Alaska. Other than Marcy, they were the only family, with Gary conspicuously absent.

It was hard to refrain from asking Marcy where her only son was on this one night when he should be standing by her side, giving her the strength necessary to get through the loss of her husband.

The line of mourners included many important people from town as well as several of the classmates Rhonda interviewed regarding the murder of Pete Potter. While Marcy seemed inconsolable, Allison was more reserved, occasionally leaning heavily against her husband for support. The fact Jackson and Cindy sat in the front row of the assembled chairs wasn't lost on either Rhonda or Bob.

"Can you say clinging vines?" Bob whispered in Rhonda's ear. "I expected them to be here, but they do look like they're ready to pounce if Marcy needs their support."

"That's what friends do," Rhonda whispered back. She wondered if she really meant the words.

By the time the visitation ended, Rhonda was more than ready to leave the funeral home. The last of the mourners had no more than left, than Jackson and Cindy hurried to Marcy's side and rushed her out the door, leaving Allison and her husband alone.

"Vultures," Allison said loud enough for Rhonda to hear. "They couldn't wait to get her out of here and leave us alone. I've only been home a couple of days. Don't they think I want some time with my mother?"

Rhonda and Bob exchanged knowing glances. "Is there anything I can do to help?" Rhonda asked.

The tears she'd expected to see the young woman shed during the visitation now ran down her cheeks.

"There's nothing anyone can do to help. I only came back here because of Dad. Mom and I have never gotten along. I don't know why now would be any different. She's always had time for Jackson and Cindy, but she could care less about me. After tomorrow, I'm going to be leaving Wisconsin and I have no plans to come back for any reason whatsoever."

"What is the connection between your folks and the Hayes family?"

Allison glanced up at her husband.

"Go ahead honey, tell them what they want to know. They have a job to do and it's best if they have all the facts."

Allison took a deep breath. "Dad and Jackson were always good friends, but I think it's turned into more than that over the years. Mom and Dad didn't think I knew about it, but they were actively swinging with Jackson and Cindy. I was old enough to know what was going on when Mom lost a baby. She wasn't very far along. She had a miscarriage and from what I figured out, the baby didn't belong to Dad. I remember when Mom talked him into having a vasectomy. When she found out she was pregnant, I overheard her talking to Cindy. She said she thought Jackson had been fixed and wasn't happy to find herself in a family way, especially since Dad couldn't give her any more children."

"After that did, they stay close?"

"Oh, yes, they were thick as thieves. Their friendships always came before Gary and me."

"That's something I wondered about, where is your brother?"

"I'd like to know the answer to that one myself. Mom said she couldn't get in touch with him. I honestly didn't think she even tried, but I called his cell phone and was told the number was no longer in service. For some reason he's turned it off. I can't help but wonder if this is his way of breaking contact with all of us."

"How do you feel about him being gay?" Bob asked.

"For me his sexual preference is his own choice. I refuse to judge him because of it, even if Mom did. Dad wasn't any more accepting. I think he felt it was like a slap in the face. If the truth be known, if Dad hadn't fallen in love with Mom, I think he might have gone the same way. There were a lot of times when I wondered if he was gay or straight, especially when so many people were coming out of the closet."

"Do you think there's any reason your brother would want your father out of the way?"

"I hate to say anything to put Gary in a bad light, but I think he blames Dad because he's gay. When he was in high school, he told me he was the way he was because of Dad. It was always hard for him to accept the fact Dad stayed at home and did the housework as well as taking care of the two of us. It was hard for me too, when my friends all had fathers who were supporting their families."

"You were well taken care of, weren't you?" Rhonda asked.

"Of course we were, but money isn't everything. I would have been thrilled if they would have taken us on a family vacation or even down to Great America, but Mom was always too busy at work and socializing and Dad didn't seem to understand the concept of going on vacation when he had a nice home."

The picture Allison was painting was so different from what David and Marcy seemed to portray, it took Rhonda a moment to comprehend what was being said.

"Thank you for your time," Bob finally said, breaking the awkward silence. "Again, please accept our condolences."

Rhonda watched as Allison and her husband left the viewing area of the funeral home. "Well, that was enlightening," she commented.

"It certainly was. I do wish we knew where to look for Gary Olson. Just having him out there is a threat."

"I don't feel quite so threatened after reading the note that was left at the Olson home. I believe the attack on David was the end of his rage."

Chapter Eighteen

Rhonda paid close attention to the conversations going on at the luncheon after David's funeral. Among the classmates who were in attendance, she heard a lot of speculation about the relationship between the Olson and Hayes families.

"I can't believe the way Jackson is fawning over Marcy," Geri commented to Mike Krumpy. "I mean, what's he trying to do, get into her pants before David's body is even cold?"

"I don't think he's too worried about something like that," Mike replied. "The gossip around town was when they were living right next door to each other it was like musical beds where those two couples were concerned. I'm more concerned about why David's son wasn't here. I looked for him last night at the visitation and again today, but the kid doesn't seem to be anywhere to be found."

Around the room other comments were made, all questioning the relationship between the two couples that were now a threesome and seemed inseparable.

"Can I talk to you?" Allison asked, taking Rhonda aside.

"Of course, is there somewhere we can go where we could have some privacy?" Rhonda asked.

"There's a small office upstairs."

Rhonda followed Allison up the stairs from the basement community room of the church to a small room just off the sanctuary.

"I had a call from Gary last night after we got to the hotel."

Rhonda inhaled deeply. "Did he tell you where he was?"

"He just said he wanted to let me know he was okay and to tell me good-bye. I asked him where he was and he said it didn't matter. He told me he's met the love of his life and they're planning to go to a state where they can be married."

"Do you have the number he called from?"

"I thought it might be something you wanted and so I copied it down from my phone."

Allison handed Rhonda a piece of paper with the logo of the hotel where they were staying on it. It was entirely possible this would be an untraceable cell phone, but there was always a chance someone at the department might be able to trace it.

"May I ask why you're staying at a hotel?"

"To be honest, I wasn't invited to stay at my mother's house. She told me when I joined the military, against her wishes, I was no longer welcome to come back home. This is the first time I've been back since high school graduation."

"What did your mother want you to do?"

"She wanted me to go to law school. She said I would never be lucky enough to find a man like my father who would be supportive of my continuing my education. I think she always regretted getting pregnant with me before they got married."

"You're older than Gary?"

The realization Allison was the older of the two came as a surprise. From what Marcy told her Gary was her oldest child. Was it possible she'd disowned her only daughter?

"I'm twenty-four, two years older than Gary. Mom and Dad got carried away right after they graduated from high school, and I was the product of that union."

For the first time, Rhonda actually studied Allison. The resemblance to Marcy was very strong but for the life of her, she could see nothing of David in this attractive young woman. What she did see was the green eyes of Jackson Hayes staring back at her.

"I hate to cut this short," Allison said, breaking the silence of the pause in the conversation. "My husband and I have to catch a bus to get us to Chicago for our flight back to Anchorage. If you need to get in touch with me, here is my contact information."

Rhonda looked down at a note written on the same paper as the one with the number from which Gary called his sister. "Thank you. I'll be sure to keep you posted about the investigation into your father's murder."

~ * ~

"So, what did you learn from the daughter?" Bob asked as they drove back to the office.

"Other than she may be Marcy's daughter, but David wasn't her biological father, I got a number I need traced."

"Whoa, back up. Did she tell you David wasn't her father?"

"No, but I studied her intently and if we were to do a DNA test, I think we'd find Jackson Hayes fathered her. From what Marcy said, I thought Gary was the oldest, but Allison told me she is two years older than her brother and the pregnancy was the reason her parents got married right after graduation. I have a feeling Marcy was messing around with both David and Jackson and David got tagged to be her loving husband. Do we know how old the Hayes kids are?"

"We must have it in the file, somewhere. That's something we can check out at the office once we get back. Now what was it you said about getting a number traced?"

"Gary called Allison last night. He didn't tell her where he was, but he said he'd met the love of his life, and he was calling to tell her good-bye. Luckily, she copied down the number from the caller ID on her phone. If the gods are smiling on us, it will be a traceable number and not a cell phone."

Once back at the office, Rhonda went through the file on the three murders while Bob took the number down to the research department to have it traced.

Rather than looking at the bulging paper file, Rhonda pulled up the information she was looking for on her computer. Under the heading of Brandon Hayes, she found what she was looking for. Brandon was the middle child. His older brother William was twenty-four, Brandon was twenty-two and Melissa was twenty. If this information was right, Jackson had been a very busy boy right after he graduated from high school.

"What did you find?" Bob asked when he returned to the office.

"William Hayes and Allison were both born the same year. Something tells me William is older and when Marcy found out she was pregnant, Jackson and Cindy were already planning to get married. The next, most logical candidate to be Allison's father was David, who was probably fooling around with Marcy at the same time as Jackson."

Before Bob could comment on Rhonda's assumptions, his phone rang. "Were you able to trace the number I brought down to you?"

He wrote something on the scratch pad Rhonda kept on her desk. "Thank you."

"It looks like we've found where Gary made the call from. The number is listed to an Andre Franklin in Oshkosh. I think we should talk to Sheriff Cantwell about this one. We need to go up there and talk to this kid."

"I agree. We could have the police department try to locate him and bring him in before we get there."

"Did I hear my name mentioned?" Sheriff Cantwell asked as he stepped into Rhonda's cubicle.

"We have a lead on Gary Olson. His sister received a call from him last night and she gave Rhonda the number at the funeral. We tracked it down and found it listed to someone named Andre Franklin in Oshkosh. We need to go up there and talk to him, but we'd like the police up there to detain him until we can get there."

"You've got a good idea. I'll make sure the garage gets your car gassed up while you contact the authorities up there."

Rhonda placed the call while Bob faxed up the photo along with the information as to why they were looking for Gary.

"We're taking a chance just driving up there. What if they can't find him?" Rhonda asked.

"He was there last night. If we don't find him, we will find his friend Andre and maybe he can give us some insight as to where Gary is."

Rhonda was relieved when Bob took the wheel. She needed this down time to think about not only the case but also her future. She knew the promotion Mark received was what he wanted, but she would miss the beauty of the Wisconsin countryside. She could hardly fathom living in a desert community.

Her mind still swirled when the ringing of the phone jolted her back to reality. "Pohs here," she answered.

"Rhonda," a shaky female voice answered. "This is Cindy Hayes.

Can I come in and talk to you?"

"Right now, I'm on my way to Oshkosh to check into a lead on the investigation. Can I meet with you tomorrow morning?"

Cindy sniffed loudly. "I can be at your office by nine."

"Is there something I can do for you now?"

"Not really. I'm staying at the Holiday Inn Express."

"Will you be in all night?"

"I'm not going anywhere. I can't, I'm too ashamed."

"I'll stop over tonight right after we get back from Oshkosh."

She no more than broke the connection than Bob's phone rang. Since he was driving, Rhonda answered it. "Pohs here."

"I was calling for Detective Masters. Have the two of you left to come up here?"

"We're about halfway to Oshkosh. Is there a problem?"

"We went to the Franklin house right after we got your fax. It seems we missed Olson by about an hour. We did a search of the house. The owner of the house said his son, Cal, and Gary had just left. He said they were talking about going to Canada. I've alerted the checkpoints at the border. They'll arrest the two of them and hold them for us. When he's in custody, we'll call you to come back up. There's nothing you can do here right now."

Rhonda felt completely defeated. "We might as well turn around," she said once she hung up the phone. "We were about an hour too late. Gary is headed toward Canada with his friend, Cal Franklin. The Oshkosh police have contacted the border patrol to detain them and hold Gary for us. They'll take care of the paperwork on that end."

"I wish I had something more concrete about the Olson kid."

"You've got my hunch," Rhonda replied.

"I was thinking along the lines of a warrant for his arrest rather than wanting to talk to him as a person of interest. What was the other call you received?"

"It was Cindy Hayes. She wants to meet with us. Something isn't right in paradise, if you know what I mean. She's staying at the Holiday Inn Express in town. We're close enough we can be there in about an hour."

Rhonda checked her phone and found the number where Cindy's call originated and hit the dial button.

"Cindy, this is Rhonda Pohs. We were following a lead that didn't pan out. Are you going to be at the hotel in about an hour?"

"Yes, I'll be here. I'm in room 216. I'll see you then."

"I wish we were closer to home," Rhonda commented once she finished the call. "Cindy sounds like she's ready to fall into a heap. Both times I talked to her it was evident she'd been crying."

Once they reached HWY 26, they were able to up the speed limit to sixty-five and bypass every small town from Juneau to Milton with the exception of Johnson Creek. With traffic being light, they pulled into the parking lot of the Holiday Inn Express in record time.

Cindy answered their knock almost immediately. Her appearance came as a real surprise to Rhonda. The perfectly applied make-up she'd come to expect was smudged and streaked with tears.

"May we come in?" Bob asked.

"Of course. I'm so pleased you were able to come and talk to me tonight."

"Why are you staying here?"

"I can't continue to live the lie anymore."

"What do you mean?"

"Back in high school, Jackson was the guy every girl wanted to go out with. I was a year older than he was and when I came home for summer vacation from college, I was thrilled when he asked me out on a date. What I wasn't prepared for was that he demanded sex before he took me back home. I'd been experimenting in college, but I didn't know Jackson well enough for a serious relationship. Two months later, I learned I was pregnant. My parents insisted Jackson and I had to get married. I wasn't thrilled, but what else could I do?"

"It must not have been too bad, the two of you are still married," Rhonda commented.

"It's been a real sham for the last few years. After we got married Marcy came over and told Jackson she was pregnant and asked what he was going to do about it. I was shocked. I didn't know Jackson had been with Marcy at the same time he'd been with me. It was David who stepped up and said he'd marry Marcy and become the father to her child. We were struggling so when David said he didn't expect Jackson to support the baby, we were relieved. Considering Marcy and David lived right next door, Jackson was able to see Allison whenever we were together and she and William grew up as best friends, just like David and Jackson had been. When Gary was born, we hoped the friendship between him and our son Brandon would be just as strong, but they didn't mesh, especially after they got older, and Gary announced he wasn't interested in girls."

Rhonda made notes quickly, while Bob held the digital recorder to get every word. "During your marriage were you and Jackson involved with the Olsons?" Rhonda asked.

"I always knew Marcy was the one Jackson really wanted to be with, but I was the one who got pregnant first. It didn't leave him much choice in the matter. We started swinging with David and Marcy right after William and Allison were born. While Jackson was a demanding lover, David was one of the sweetest men in the world. I was always more fulfilled after being with him."

"Are you sure your other kids belong to Jackson?"

"Positive. We were always very careful, and David and Jackson always wore condoms when we were swinging.

"After we had Brandon and David and Marcy had Gary, David decided to have a vasectomy. I took care of his kids when he went to the hospital. I know Marcy was busy with school, so Jackson took him to the hospital. It was a godsend for me, since we were still swinging, and David no longer needed to use a condom. That was when Marcy turned up pregnant. I knew it wasn't David's, but I kept my mouth shut. Jackson said as long as he didn't take responsibility for the baby, he wouldn't get saddled with child support we couldn't afford because I was also expecting. Don't get me wrong, but it was a blessing when Marcy miscarried."

"How did Jackson feel about the miscarriage?" Bob asked.

"He was relieved as well. Even though David said he'd raise the child just like he was raising Allison, Jackson was concerned that one day he'd decide to chuck the whole thing and dump Marcy and the kids on our doorstep."

"You mentioned something about Brandon and Gary not getting along. Can you elaborate on it?" Rhonda pressed.

"When they were little, they were great friends. When they got older, things changed. Brandon played football, but Gary was too small for the game. He didn't like to hear Brandon talk about football practice and said he'd rather hang out with Michelle and play with her dolls than listen to some jock spouting off about his exploits on the football team. It really hurt Brandon's feelings. Shortly after that, Marcy said she needed to live in town, so she'd be closer to her job. They'd made quite a bit of money by subdividing the farm and I'm sure Marcy wanted that trophy house in one of the exclusive neighborhoods. Of course, it also meant the Olson kids would have to change schools. Gary was a freshman, so it didn't bother him too much, but Allison was a junior at Clinton, and she didn't want to leave. Marcy pulled some strings, so Allison could continue with her class."

Rhonda's head spun with all the information spilling from Cindy's lips. "How is it you're here?"

More tears ran down Cindy's cheeks. "After the funeral, Jackson and I had a huge fight. He told me he'd only married me because I was pregnant, and Marcy was the woman he really loved. I told him the two of them deserve each other. Marcy has always been a bitch and without David as a buffer, I honestly don't want to be around her. He stormed out of the house, and I came here."

"Won't he be able to track you down?"

"Not for a while. I've always kept a separate account in my name, including my own credit card. You see, I've been considering divorce for quite some time. With what I've saved I'll be all right and Wisconsin is a community property state, so if he wants Marcy, he'll have to pay me through the nose."

"Do you have any idea who was involved in any of these murders?" Rhonda asked.

More tears flowed from Cindy's eyes. "I don't have any proof, but if I had to name someone who wanted David and Brandon dead it would be Gary. That poor kid took a terrible ribbing once he came out and admitted to being gay. On more than one occasion, I heard Brandon call him Gary the Fairy. The name stuck and I'm certain it followed him to his new school. There seemed to be a lot of bad blood between the two of them. As for David, even though he was an excellent lover, I always had the feeling he'd be just as happy with a man as he was with a woman. I heard an argument between David and Gary. I think Gary blamed his father for his being gay. To be truthful, I always thought both of those kids were ashamed of the fact their father wasn't the brightest bulb in the box and he only worked menial jobs, while their mother was a big hot shot lawyer."

"Are you telling us you think Gary is behind the last two murders?" Rhonda questioned.

Inside her mind, having her suspicions confirmed by Cindy was setting off warning lights. They had to get back to the office and have a warrant issued for Gary Olson in connection with the deaths of both Brandon Hayes and David Olson.

~ * ~

"That was interesting," Bob said as they pulled away from the hotel. "Do you think Jackson and Marcy are already together?"

"I doubt it. Unless it was all a big act, I think Marcy actually loved David. It's possible she loves Jackson too, but in her position, she has to think about her image. She has a really high-profile job. It wouldn't do her reputation any good to bury her husband of almost twenty-five years one day and be seen with her lover the next."

"I know it's been a long day. As much as I'd like to take you home so you can have some alone time with Mark, we have to get back to the office and have Cantwell issue an arrest warrant for Gary Olson."

~ * ~

By the time Bob dropped Rhonda off at home it was almost six. Noticing Mark's truck in the driveway made her anxious to get inside and shut out the twists and turns this day had taken.

As soon as she opened the front door, she saw Mark out on the deck working at the grill. "What's for supper?" she called.

"I picked up some fresh salmon and have it ready to put on the grill. I'm also grilling some vegetables and I've made a killer dill sauce. I'm glad you're finally home. By the time you get comfortable I'll have everything ready to eat."

Rhonda made her way to the bedroom and eyed the bed with longing. She was tired but the rumbling of her stomach told her it had been several hours since she attended the funeral luncheon at the church. Even though it hadn't been that long ago, it seemed like it was eons since she'd last eaten. Of course, at those things she was more interested in mingling with those attending than in actually partaking of the amount of food filling her plate.

She smiled to see the table on the deck set with her colorful summer plates as well as glasses of white wine. "This looks beautiful," she said as Mark held her chair for her.

"I thought you needed something special. This has been one hell of a week."

"It certainly has. I can't believe it's only been three weeks since Pete Potter was found dead out at the Hayes farm."

"Are you any closer to an arrest on this one?"

"Not really. We have some good leads, but we can't seem to find our top suspect. I'm afraid I'll be still working on this one when you have to leave for Las Vegas."

"Well, I do have some good news about the move," Mark said after taking his first sip of wine. "The realtor called me this afternoon and we have a showing of the house tomorrow."

"Oh, so that's why we're eating outside. You don't want to mess up your clean kitchen."

They shared a good laugh until the house phone rang.

"Am I interrupting supper?" Phil asked.

"We're just starting. How goes the vacation?"

"I've survived being with Judy's sister and her husband for an entire week. We were getting ready to head out for Las Vegas and I thought I'd touch base and find out what's going on with your case."

Rhonda took a deep breath. "Today was David Olson's funeral."

"David Olson? No, what happened?"

"He was attacked and beaten. He came around for a while but didn't make it."

"Do you think all three murders are connected?"

"You know I do. We have a suspect, but at this moment, he's

disappeared. We think he might be heading for Canada, so we're hopeful the border patrol will be able to stop him before he gets out of the country."

"I wish I was there to help you on this one. How's Martin doing?"

"The last I heard he was home from the hospital. On the night of Brandon Hayes' murder, he suffered an attack of appendicitis. On that same night Bob Masters' partner was in an auto accident, so Bob and I are working on this one. He's got the experience, but I think he's having a problem getting used to working with me. I'm sure you can sympathize with him."

They talked for several more minutes, before Mark brought the salmon to the table.

Chapter Nineteen

"Are you up?" Bob greeted Rhonda when she answered her phone.

"Barely, Mark and I are just having our breakfast."

"Good, then you should be done by the time I get there. Last night, after we got back, Sheriff Cantwell issued an arrest warrant for Gary Olson as a person of interest. The information we got from Cindy Hayes was enough to convince Cantwell that Gary could be our guy, at least in his father's murder. This morning, we received a call saying he's been detained in Sault Ste. Marie when he tried to cross the border into Canada without a passport. We're expected at the airport. They've assigned us that young deputy, Alex Hartman, from yesterday, to go up there and arrest him."

"Will I at least have time to finish my breakfast?"

"Don't see why not. It should take me at least half an hour to pick up Alex and get to your place. Then we can go out to the airport. There's a plane and pilot waiting for us."

Rhonda ended the call and sighed deeply. "Duty calls. I've got a half an hour to finish breakfast and put on my face."

"Your face looks great to me," Mark said, leaning over the table to kiss her. "Just calm down, hopefully Bob will be late."

Rhonda smiled. "You're right. I have plenty of time. There's no reason to rush through my omelet."

"So, what's up now?"

"We have to fly up to Sault Ste. Marie and pick up a prisoner."

"You mean the guy you were talking to Phil about last night?"

"The same one. After yesterday, we believe he's responsible for at least one if not all three of the murders. If our hunch is right, I could be putting in my notice sooner than I anticipated."

"Do you think we could get lucky enough to have the showing of the house turn into a sale? If so, we could be leaving for Las Vegas early and have the extra time to get settled."

Rhonda relaxed. Maybe this time things will go smoothly. and they could come to an end with the three murders plaguing her life for the past three weeks.

~ * ~

The flight from the Rock County Airport in the small county plane went smoothly. At first Rhonda questioned why Sheriff Cantwell sent along Alex Hartman until she remembered he'd known Gary when he was in high school. Hopefully, his appearance hadn't changed so drastically he'd be unrecognizable.

She expected the overly eager young man would be asking a million questions about the case and what part they thought Gary played in the three murders they were investigating. Instead, he engaged them in polite conversation about his family and his plans to make the sheriff's department his career.

"I had a call from Phil last night," Rhonda said when there was a lull in the conversation.

"Phil Mason?" the young deputy questioned. "I heard he took a position in Madison. He's the reason I joined the force. As a matter of fact, he gave me a recommendation for this job."

"How do you know Phil?" Rhonda asked.

"My folks own the duplex where Phil and Judy lived when they first got married. Mom and Dad lived on the other side and Mom and Judy got to be good friends. The last time I was home, Mom told me how much Judy was looking forward to driving out to California. I hope they're having a good time."

"Oh, I think they are. At least Phil sounded more relaxed than I've heard him sound in a long time."

"That's right, Phil was your partner for a while."

"So," Bob asked Rhonda, "was good old Phil chomping at the bit to get back here and into the investigation?"

"I think he'd give anything to be in on this one but there are two things we tend to forget. The first is, he's no longer with the sheriff's office and the second, he's well acquainted with at least two of the victims and was there for the first murder. If that doesn't shout hand's off, I don't know what does."

"I heard about that class reunion," Alex commented. "I can understand him knowing Mr. Potter and Mr. Olson, but how would he have known the Hayes kid?"

"We all had a nodding acquaintance with Brandon," Rhonda said. "It was his recording studio we used for our interrogation of the classmates on the weekend of Pete Potter's murder. It wasn't until last night when everything started falling into place, everything that is, except Pete Potter. I'm not really sure how he plays in the picture of this whole thing."

It didn't take long for them to land and be met by the local police. Since Gary hadn't been able to cross over into Canada, he was in the custody of the Michigan authorities.

Rhonda sat with Bob in the interrogation room when Gary was brought in. Rather than the clean-cut teenager she saw in the yearbook photo, the young man looked very unkempt. His long hair was tied back with a rubber band showing off more piercings than anyone should have. Beside the seven earrings in each ear, both eyebrows were pierced, as were his cheeks, nose and lower lip. She didn't have to be a detective to visualize what other body parts might have been pierced in the name of art. Along with the piercings, were the numerous tattoos adorning his neck and what parts of his arms were visible beneath his tee shirt, with an obscene saying emblazoned across the front.

"Gary Olson, I'm Detective Rhonda Pohs."

"Well, bully for you. Just why in the hell did you have me arrested? Since when is it a big deal to cross the border without a passport?"

Rhonda stared directly into Gary's blue eyes and could easily see a young David Olson within them. "Since we have a warrant for your arrest for the murders of David Olson and Brandon Hayes. I must tell you; you have the right…"

"Yah, I know all about that Miranda crap. I should, those bastards told me the same thing when they arrested me yesterday and wouldn't tell me what I was charged with. Do you really think I offed my old man?"

"We have enough evidence to believe you did. We also think you're the one responsible for Brandon Hayes' murder."

"If you think I'm going to talk to you about any of the shit going on back home, you're wrong. I'll wait for my public defender."

"Public defender?" Rhonda questioned. "Not someone in your mother's firm?"

"I want nothing to do with that fuckin' bitch. She slept her way from being a pregnant teenager to being a top lawyer. I'd rather be dead than have anything to do with her or her firm."

~ * ~

The flight back from Michigan was extremely tense. As soon as Gary asked for a lawyer any mention of the reason for the warrant for his arrest went against protocol.

The silence within the cabin of the plane gave Rhonda time to contemplate the reason for all of these senseless murders. From what Cindy said last night, it was entirely possible Gary blamed David for his sexual orientation. In her rational mind, Rhonda couldn't understand why anyone would kill a parent over the hand life dealt him.

Brandon's murder made sense as well. As a kid, he'd been Gary's best friend and possibly his tormentor. She wondered how being called Gary the Fairy would have affected his psyche growing up.

The only things that didn't add up were Pete Potter's murder as well as the acts of vandalism to her home.

By the time they returned to the office, the public defender waited for them in the interrogation room. Rhonda and Bob went back to their offices while the lawyer met with his client.

"My baby," Marcy shouted as she stormed into Rhonda's office only moments after their arrival. "I've been told you have my baby here. I demand to know what's going on with him. I want to see my son."

"Sit down Marcy," Rhonda began. "Gary has made it perfectly clear he doesn't want you anywhere near him. He's meeting with his lawyer right now."

"His lawyer? Who in the hell is his lawyer? I should be defending him from whatever trumped up charges you have against him."

"I'm afraid your son made it abundantly clear he wants you to have nothing to do with his case."

"Just what have you charged him with?"

"We have enough information to charge him with the murder of both your husband and Brandon Hayes."

Rhonda watched as the color drained from Marcy's face. From her expression, Rhonda knew Marcy wasn't as surprised as she let on. Something was going on and Rhonda intended to get to the bottom of it.

Before Rhonda could say more, Marcy stormed out of the cubicle and rushed down the hall toward the interrogation room. Although Rhonda followed as quickly as she could, Marcy entered the room just as Rhonda arrived.

"Get your ass out of here," she shouted at the public defender who'd been conferring with Gary. "This is my son and I'll be the one to defend him. You know I'm the best lawyer in this county, in this whole damn state for that matter."

"I don't want anything to do with you, bitch," Gary spat. "If it hadn't been for you and your lover none of this would have ever happened."

"Shut your mouth. As your lawyer, to say nothing of being your mother, I'm telling you not to say another word."

"You may be my mother, but I made it perfectly clear I didn't want you as my lawyer. How in the hell can you hope to defend me when I was just doing what you wanted me to do?"

Before anyone could stop her, Marcy lunged at her son, clasping both hands around Gary's throat and squeezing with a death grip. It took all of Rhonda and Bob's combined strength to pull her off and get her out of the room.

"Just remember, you little bastard, keep your fuckin' mouth shut. You go talking any nonsense and you can kiss whatever inheritance you thought you'd be getting goodbye."

"I don't want your fuckin' money. In fact, I think it's time to tell the truth about everything that's happened these past few weeks. I may be going down for these murders, but I refuse to go down alone."

Marcy struggled against Bob and Rhonda as they rushed her to another interrogation room.

"What was that all about?" Bob demanded once the door closed behind them.

"You can't believe anything that little bastard tells you. He's just like his father, a complete wimp. Why else would he look like he does and say he prefers men rather than women in bed? He wasn't raised like that."

Rhonda noticed Marcy's eyes were glazed over like those of a mad woman. She decided to leave Bob to handle the irate lawyer while she went back to the interrogation room where the public defender and one of the deputies were trying to calm down Gary.

"I'm glad to see you, Detective Pohs," the lawyer said. "Against my advice, my client wants to tell you about the murders you've been investigating."

"Are you certain that's what you want to do, Gary?" Rhonda asked.

In an instant, the tattooed kid before her went from belligerent suspect to a confused young man.

"Let's start with Pete Potter. What do you know about his murder?"

"Good old Sneaky Pete. For as long as I can remember he's been dogging my mother, trying to get into her pants. To make matters worse, he put my dad down every chance he got. Mom thought it was best if I went to school in Madison. My dad was so proud of the fact I got accepted at UW. It was a good place for me. You know, I could be with people like me. One night I went out with my friends and ran into Sneaky Pete all dolled up like a woman. It's one thing to be gay and another to dress up like something you aren't. My friends and I gave him a real hard time especially when he didn't recognize me with my tattoos. Of course, him being as drunk as a skunk didn't help matters much."

"Did you do anything else?"

"Hell no, it was all in fun, until Mom came up to Madison on business and stopped at my apartment. I told her about meeting him and she asked me what I thought of his lifestyle. I said I thought it stunk but to each his own. Then she told me he was threatening to blackmail her if she didn't go to bed with him and she would sure like him out of the way. It was dear old Mom who told me about the reunion and that Pete would be there. Mom offered me twenty grand if I'd kill him. She even suggested stuffing the panties down his throat, so he'd suffocate, then dumping him in the lake. That was her idea too. She wanted to make you think there was a serial killer on the loose. I smashed your window with the note and vandalized your backyard, but I never meant you any harm."

"What about Brandon Hayes?"

"Brandon was a real piss ant. We were friends until I came out of the closet. As soon as that happened, he was my worst enemy. I knew Mom was banging his old man, hell I even found out Jackson Hayes was Allison's father. Mom told me the only thing standing between her and Jackson being happy was his wife, Cindy. She told me she didn't think Brandon was Jackson's kid. He was like Allison, some other guy's brat, probably my father's. She said if Brandon was out of the way, Cindy would fall apart and give Jackson the reason he'd been looking for to get a divorce."

"That just leaves your father."

"Mom wanted him out of the way too, but she was afraid of what people would say. I always blamed him for the way I am. I think the note I left there said it all. He was the beginning and the end. I wish he'd never fathered me, but once he was dead it was over. I was going to Canada to live where I didn't have to deal with any of it. I figured I'd given my mother a favor by getting the old man out of the way and sending Cindy over the edge by getting rid of Brandon. I planned to call her when I got to Canada and get her to send me the money, she'd promised in exchange for me being quiet about why I did those three murders."

"Once I have this transcribed, I'll bring your statement back in for your signature."

"I'd like to talk to the district attorney about a deal," the public defender said.

"That's between you and the district attorney. Your client is facing three murder charges, plus two more for vandalism. I don't know how much leniency you can bargain for."

Before going back to the interrogation room where Bob was dealing with Marcy, Rhonda went to Sheriff Cantwell's office.

"That was quite a confession you got from the Olson kid," he greeted her. "I watched it and listened to every word. Once we get it typed up and signed, we'll have this case just about closed."

"What about Marcy Olson? She might not have done the actual murders, but I think she's as guilty as her son."

"I agree, that's why I'm getting a warrant for her arrest. Something tells me you want to be the one to carry it out."

Rhonda nodded. This had been her case from the get-go, but she never expected things to turn out this way. Thinking back to her original interview with Marcy Olson, she'd had her suspicions, but the lawyer in Marcy came out, convincing Rhonda that although Pete Potter threatened Marcy and David with blackmail, neither of them took the threat seriously. Now it seemed as though the threat was real and loomed on the horizon as something that could ruin her plans for the future with Jackson.

"I'd like to have Jackson Hayes brought in again," Rhonda said. "It's possible he was in on this."

Chapter Twenty

Marcy paced the interrogation room like a caged tiger. Bob stood looking at her through the two-way mirror. "What went on in there?" he asked.

"Gary confessed to everything, but he implicated Marcy as the person who orchestrated the whole thing. I have the go ahead from Cantwell to arrest her for conspiracy to murder Pete, Brandon and David. At her insistence, Gary killed Pete with the promise of twenty thousand dollars being transferred to his account so he could move to Canada. Of course, Mommy Dearest wasn't happy with just one murder, she suggested the other two as well. She knew there was bad blood between Gary and Brandon. She also knew Gary resented his father."

"Are you going to arrest her?"

"What do you think?"

Rhonda turned and went into the interrogation room.

"Well, it's about time you got back to me," Marcy spat. "I've got half a mind to sue you for false imprisonment."

Rhonda took a deep breath. "Marcy Olson, you are under arrest for conspiracy to commit murder in the cases of Peter Potter, Brandon Hayes and David Olson."

"You are one insane psycho bitch. What did that little bastard tell you? Whatever it was I don't know how you can believe a little homo like him."

"Settle down Marcy. I need to read you your rights. "You have the right to remain silent, anything you say can and will be used against you in a court of law. You are entitled to an attorney, if you cannot afford one, one will be…"

"How dare you? What do you mean if I cannot afford a lawyer? I'm Marcy Olson, one of the top lawyers in this town. Of course, I can afford a lawyer. I'll act as my own counsel and as so I have decided not to say anything more to you."

"I doubt if you need to say anything to us Marcy," Sheriff Cantwell said, as he entered the room. "I heard your son's statement, and from that it's evident you were the mastermind behind the murders happening in this county. I have a female officer who will be escorting you to the booking area."

Marcy gave Rhonda a stare that screamed cold-blooded murderer. Rather than tears and hysterics, she remained calm.

"You, Detective Pohs, will live to regret what you're doing to me. I'll be filing a suit of harassment against you and this entire department. You have no idea who you are arresting under such false pretenses. I'm well known in the legal community and …"

"Please come with me, Mrs. Olson," a female deputy said as she entered the room.

Rhonda stepped aside as Marcy was led away from interrogation to where the prisoners went through intake.

"Marcy, what the hell is going on here? Why is she in handcuffs?" Jackson said as he entered the area.

Rhonda saw Cindy Hayes enter behind her husband.

"It looks like your sweetie is being arrested."

"Marcy had nothing to do with this. It was that fag son of hers. He murdered Pete because he didn't want his mother to have to sleep with that sleaze bag."

"Just how do you know that Mr. Hayes?" Rhonda inquired.

"Marcy and I were talking, and she told me what she thought. Pete was threatening her and…"

"You knew about this, and you didn't come to us, Mr. Hayes?" Bob asked. "I think you should not say anything more until you get a lawyer."

"Am I under arrest?"

"For right now, there are no charges pending, but that doesn't mean they couldn't be filed later in the investigation."

"Could I talk to you, in private?" Cindy inquired.

Rhonda nodded toward the now empty interrogation room.

"What is it you want to tell me, Cindy?" Rhonda could see the events of the day had taken a toll on Cindy.

"I went back out to the farm this morning. Jackson and Marcy didn't see me, but I heard what they were saying. They were talking about Pete's murder. Jackson said he didn't know why Marcy wasn't content with killing off Pete, why did she have to turn on Brandon. She told him she'd decided Brandon's death would drive me over the edge. Once I'd been committed, he could divorce me, and they could be together."

"What about David?" Rhonda asked.

"Jackson told her he knew David would never give her a divorce, so that was why they had to make sure he was out of the way as well."

"Are you saying your husband was in on all this?"

Cindy hung her head. "I'm sure he was from the beginning. Just before we decided to host the reunion, Pete stopped out at the house. The only reason I knew about his visit was I was just getting home when he was leaving. Jackson told me Pete came out to arrange for us to have the reunion at the farm, but I knew differently."

"Why would you say that?"

"Marcy isn't the only woman Jackson's been catting around with. I've known for years he's been screwing everything in a skirt in town. In reality, he's not much better than Pete in that respect. I thought he was being a little more discreet, but apparently, I wasn't the only one who knew about it. I helped out on the committee and Pete said a few things that didn't make sense. I started putting two and two together. I might not be a lawyer, but after I overheard Marcy and Jackson talking today, everything seemed to fall into place. Just before I decided to leave, Marcy got a call on her cell. I couldn't hear what she was saying, but when she hung up, she told Jackson she had to get down here before Gary opened his big mouth and screwed everything up."

"Thank you, Cindy. All of this information will be of help."

"Do I have to see him again?"

"Not today. If you stay here, I'll go out and arrest him. I'm afraid the only ones who were innocent in this whole mess were you and David. Thank goodness they didn't go so far as to kill you as well. I think Allison, as well as your surviving children, will need you to be strong now."

~ * ~

As soon as Rhonda stepped into the hall, she could hear Jackson shouting. Along with his rant, she could hear Marcy all the way from the interrogation area.

"What did Cindy have to say?" Sheriff Cantwell asked.

"She told me enough to arrest Jackson for conspiracy to commit murder in the cases of Pete Potter and David Olson. It seems like he was in on it from the very beginning, because Pete was blackmailing Jackson for his behavior, just like he was blackmailing Marcy."

"It's your collar, Rhonda. You make the arrest."

Rhonda walked down to the hall to where Jackson was shouting at Bob. "Jackson Hayes, please put your hands behind your back. You are under arrest for conspiracy to commit murder in the cases of Pete Potter and David Olson."

Jackson sobered and hung his head while Rhonda read him his rights.

"What did that bitch tell you? A wife can't testify against her husband. Besides, she doesn't know diddly squat about anything. Whatever she told you is out of vengeance because I told her I loved Marcy more than I did her."

"We can sort all of that out later," Sheriff Cantwell said. "For now we need to take you down to intake so we can get you fingerprinted and booked."

Chapter Twenty-One

"You've had one hell of a career with the county, Rhonda," Phil said as they sat on Mark and Rhonda's back deck. "I can't believe what started out as a fun class reunion turned into a triple homicide. I still don't know how you cracked the case."

Rhonda smiled at her former partner. "To be truthful, it was Gary who solved the case for us. I would have never put all the pieces together if it hadn't been for the note he left with his father after the beating. Literally translated, it said David was the beginning and the end. In other words David gave him life and he was prepared to end David's life. I think he hoped it would give him the money he needed to start a new life in Canada."

"So, how did you get a line on Marcy and Jackson?"

"Cindy Hayes told us she was leaving Jackson then Gary decided to spill the beans about how Marcy enlisted his help in all three murders. After Marcy's arrest, Cindy filled in all the rest of the pieces and the rest, as they say, is history."

"To think this all started with our innocent class reunion. Do you think they'll have three trials?"

"Gary took a deal for his testimony. Even though he carried out the murders, he did turn states' evidence against his mother and Jackson. He'll be eligible for parole in ten years. As for Marcy and Jackson, they pleaded guilty and were both sentenced to life without parole. It certainly saved the county the cost of a trial."

"I heard all that through the grapevine, but I wanted to hear it from you. I talked to Cindy this morning. She's already filed for divorce. Under the circumstances, her lawyer says she'll end up with everything. That makes her the owner of the farm and since William is working the land, she shouldn't have to worry about anything for the rest of her life."

Rhonda agreed. Considering the hell Cindy lived through for the past twenty-five years, she deserved to be comfortable and have some peace in her life.

"That was the realtor on the phone," Mark said coming out onto the deck. "The couple who went through the house two weeks ago put in an offer."

Rhonda took a deep breath. She knew they had the house priced to sell, but she'd heard nightmare stories about lowball offers from prospective buyers. "What's the bad news?"

"What makes you think it's all bad?"

"Well, I've heard about…"

Mark put his finger to her lips. "Don't go on what you've heard. This is a good offer. They are meeting our price and they've added an extra ten thousand for their choice of the furnishings as well as the lawn care equipment. I think it's a fair offer, considering we probably won't need the lawn mower, edger, trimmer and snow blower in Las Vegas."

Rhonda put her arms around Mark's neck and hugged him tightly. "I think it's just perfect."

"I can't believe everything is happening so quickly," Phil's wife Judy said. "I hate to see you leave town, but you've had such a marvelous offer, I can understand why you didn't turn it down."

"Face it Judy, this is Rhonda we're talking about. If you recall she's solved every case she's worked on. Whatever she touches turns into pure gold. I had no qualms about them selling the house for their asking price and making a profit in the bargain."

Rhonda laughed at Phil's statement. "I think you tend to over exaggerate things, partner."

"Over exaggeration is not one of my qualities. You know Judy and I are going to miss you guys. I guess I'm also a little jealous about you selling this place so quickly. Our place has been on the market since spring and not even a nibble. Maybe it's a sign."

"What kind of a sign, Phil?" Judy questioned. "Are you saying you're going to be content commuting?"

"I'm not thrilled with the drive, especially with winter coming. I think we should consider becoming landlords. I found a place that is on a foreclosure sale and it's not far from my new office. Since we don't owe anything on our house here it might be wise to rent it out. It's not like there's much we have to do to get it ready to rent. We've been making improvements on it ever since we put it on the market."

Mark went into the house and came out with a bottle of wine. "I think this deserves a toast. We're all embarking on new adventures, but I know we'll never be further away than e-mails and Facebook. Besides, I have a feeling Phil and Judy will be returning to Vegas and I think we can more than accommodate guests and save them the cost of going to a hotel."

Epilogue

Rhonda took one last walk through the home they were leaving. It was strange to think of the new owners using the furnishings she'd purchased over the years. Considering once they got to Las Vegas they would be buying new furniture, they had booked a hotel for two weeks until they could make Dawn's house their own.

After several long talks and a quick trip out to look over the property, they'd returned to meet with Dawn and negotiate a good price for purchasing the house they both loved the minute they did the walk through with the neighbor who was helping Dawn out with the sale.

Tears ran down Rhonda's cheeks as she put her spare key on the counter. "Are you sure we're doing the right thing, Mark?"

When he enfolded her in his arms she could feel similar tears on Mark's cheeks. "We're doing the right thing, I promise."

"I don't have a job. Are you certain we can afford to live on one income?"

"Didn't you tell me Cantwell faxed out your recommendation to the Las Vegas police force, as well as to the State Patrol, the Clark County sheriff's office and several other forces in the area? Any one of them would be foolish not to hire you once they meet you. Why don't you just relax? You can have a little fun getting acquainted with the area until you find another job. I have a feeling you'll stumble over the perfect position once we get settled."

"I guess you're right, as usual. Look how I got the job with the county. I certainly didn't apply for it. Maybe someone out there will come knocking at our door. We can only take things one day at a time and see what happens."

"Knowing you, our life in Las Vegas will be anything but boring."

Rhonda closed the door for the last time. As she slid into the passenger seat of Mark's van she dreamed about the new life they were embarking on and wondered what new adventure would be in her future.

Coming Soon
by the author at
Rogue Phoenix Press

Murder in Red Rock Canyon
The Rhonda Pohs Mysteries Book Five

Following her husband when he takes a new position, Rhonda leaves Wisconsin behind to begin a new life in Las Vegas, Nevada.

Without a job for the first time, she is thrilled when she obtains a position with the Clark County Sheriff's department. To celebrate her new job, she and her husband, Mark, go to Red Rock Canyon for a relaxing day of sightseeing.

Even before she is scheduled to begin her job, she finds herself at the center of a murder. The victim, a college student, has been killed using an ancient Native American weapon, close to the petroglyphs.

Have the ancients returned to protect their history or is there a modern-day predator trying to confuse her with the use of ancient weapons?

About the Author

Wife, mother, grandmother and great grandmother, Sherry is first and foremost an author. She and her husband of sixty years enjoy their retirement and wonder how they ever had time to work. Sherry calls her husband a saint for putting up with an author.